SEVENTEEN PARCELS

a novel by

MIC LOWTHER

Olympus Story House

TABLE OF CONTENTS

PART THREE - RECKONING

Part One – Scattering

CHAPTER 1

I Have a Client

Austin Somerfeld was famous.

He paid little attention to being famous because it arose from doing things he considered "no big deal" or "just part of the job."

Austin was a driver. He drove taxicabs and busses and limousines and semis and garbage trucks for whatever job might be available at the time, including, at present, a package delivery van. The whole famous part came about when he drove cardboard boxes containing $12 million in cash cross-country to a seedy neighborhood in Paterson, New Jersey, no questions asked.

And the time he drove an ice chest with a human heart for transplanting a thousand miles to a distant hospital in weather so bad, airports within a hundred miles of the destination were closed.

And the time he drove cages full of live rattlesnakes and cottonmouths and copperheads and coral snakes and black mambas and other seriously horrid and dream-haunting creatures to a serpentarium exhibition in downtown Manhattan.

The historical accumulation of these and other such occasions resulted in frequent requests for his services.

"Could you have Austin drive this for me?" customers would often ask. "Of course," was always the reply.

He got it done.

He delivered.

Thus, he was famous.

These lingering anecdotes might explain an invitation he received to interview for a driving job that supposedly paid a half-million dollars for work to do pretty much whenever he wanted.

Preposterous? Sounded like it.

A scam? Maybe, but how it worked might be interesting.

Too good to be true? Probably.

Nonetheless, he was curious, so he arrived at the appointed interview precisely on time. An assistant showed him directly into the law office of C. Monica Stansbury, Esq. and handed her a page of notes.

"Good afternoon," he said to a stunning mid-40s redhead with red-framed glasses and a piercing gaze. She sat behind a tidy, well-organized desk and wore a long-sleeved grey dress with a wide silver bracelet on her left wrist. A red blazer hung on a hangar on a nearby coat tree.

Her furniture was of warm, reddish wood. Windows had floor-length, grey linen draperies, and art pieces hanging in spaces between them were the puzzling abstracts often found in law offices. Fresh yellow daffodils filled a vase on her credenza. It was a look of friendly and practical utility, enough to impress but not intimidate.

It was not a corner office.

It was not on the building's top floor.

However, the directory in the hallway had shown at least 50 lawyers' names, and the only one named Stansbury in the Stansbury Law Firm was C. Monica. She was clearly in charge.

Austin had dressed for the occasion. Visiting a law office required dress pants and shoes, ironed shirt with a collar, combed hair and clean fingernails, and no baseball cap worn either frontwards or backward. A sports jacket and tie would have been overdoing it, he'd initially thought, but wouldn't have been out of place.

"Mr. Somerfeld," C. Monica responded, motioning him to sit down, "thank you for being so prompt. May I dispense with formality and call you Austin?"

He nodded but said nothing.

"According to my information," she continued, glancing at her notes, "you are 27 years old, not married, a high school graduate, you've lived your entire life here in Oklahoma City, and at the moment are employed to drive a package delivery van."

"Yes," he replied. He could add other relevant and colorful details about his life but didn't.

"Do you drive your van alone?" C. Monica went on.

He nodded.

"Do family or other obligations affect your daily schedule?"

"No," he replied, "the only thing on my schedule is work, which is flexible."

"How so?"

"The company has many drivers so I can work however much I want, a lot or a little or not at all, although sometimes I'm specifically requested."

"Yes, so I've heard. Can you follow precise directions?" she asked intently, moving on to her next topic. She did not chew gum, drum her fingers, or have other distracting mannerisms. Instead, she asked questions crisply and waited, attentive and unmoving, for an answer.

"It's my whole job," Austin replied. "Take a package to a certain address. Deliver a van-load of packages each day in an efficient sequence so they arrive on time and you're not still driving late at night."

"Can you improvise when things don't go according to plan?"

"I do so every day."

She said nothing, as if she were waiting for something more.

"I carry treats for barking dogs," Austin said, "but most drivers do that. One place I delivered to had a pet wolf loose in the yard. I went through the gate and when it approached not looking friendly, I sat down on the ground so I was about its same height and would appear less threatening. I just waited for it to get used to me. Dog treats work on wolves, it turns out. We're great buddies now."

"Sounds like quick thinking," the lawyer said. "I must say you come with an impressive history of accomplishments and recommendations which support your answers.

"Here's my last question, and please excuse me if it seems too personal: Do you have any bad habits which negatively affect your daily life?"

"Um, you mean like hanging out in bars and getting into fights, losing large amounts of cash in back-room card games, buying, selling, or using drugs?"

"Sorry, but yes."

"No, none of those, but I do have an occasional problem with driving." Austin paused.

C. Monica looked at him and silently awaited an explanation.

"I like being on the road. I like going to new places to see or do something different. But once I get a destination in mind, no place is too far away to go there. I drove 250 miles out of my way once to get an ice cream cone. Long drive, but, as it turned out, definitely worth it."

"Hmm," C. Monica said with a hint of a smile, "I must admit you have me curious. What kind of ice cream would be that compelling?"

3

"Guinness, only available in March in Savannah," Austin replied. "There are plenty of recipes on the Internet to make your own but this is the real thing."

"Perfectly understandable," she said. "So, moving on, I've asked you questions; what questions do you have of me?"

"What is the job, and what are these 'precise directions?'"

"I have a client who wants 17 parcels hidden all across the United States where they cannot be easily or accidentally found," C. Monica said. "The choice of where to hide them would be mostly up to you."

"Do I need to know what's in them?"

"No, you do not. I don't know what the parcels contain, but the client assures me there's nothing perishable, stolen, or illegal."

"And nobody lies to lawyers," Austin said.

"Everybody lies to lawyers," C. Monica replied, "but the truth always comes out."

She continued: "Guidelines or rules accompanying this assignment are primarily common sense but not written down, so listen carefully.

"Rule One: Do not open any of the parcels, not ever." She paused, waiting for his nod of understanding, then went on.

"Rule Two: Do not tell anyone, anywhere, what you are doing. Do not ask permission of anyone, anywhere, to do what you are doing.

"Rule Three: Hide parcels in a safe, anonymous place, preferably each in a different US State. Not in a bank deposit box where you must identify yourself to an institution and pay an annual fee, not in an abandoned building which might burn or be torn down, not where an animal could dig it up, not anywhere in plain sight where someone could find it and take it just out of sheer curiosity."

Austin thought about this a moment. "It limits choices somewhat but makes sense," he said.

"My client was particular about this. Don't make them easy to find; don't make them impossible to find. Put parcels where a reasonably intelligent person or persons working together could follow directions to them, but not necessarily anytime soon."

"I think I already know the answer to this question," Austin said, "but where will these directions come from?"

"From you, of course, since you'll be the only one who knows where the parcels are. But the information will be safeguarded through the next Rule.

"Rule Four: Parcels are numbered and all the same size and shape.

4

Keep a log of state, city, and precisely where you put each one, including GPS coordinates. Once you've done that, mail me a letter telling where it is, explaining relevant details, and including claim tickets or whatever might go with it. Include pictures if you think they might be helpful.

"Write the parcel number on the outside of the envelope. I'll accumulate your letters without opening them until I have all 17, then give them to my client when he asks for them."

"Sounds like setting up some sort of cross-country Easter egg hunt," Austin said. C. Monica shrugged and made a maybe-so expression.

"Rule Five:" she continued, "once you've hidden the parcel and mailed me the letter, tell me in a subsequent e-mail where to send the next parcel. I will overnight it to you there. To be clear, the letter from Rule Four is for parcel location information only and can take its time getting here. The e-mail from Rule Five is for other matters needing immediate attention."

Austin nodded his understanding.

"Rule Six: Parcels will not come to you in any order, but regardless of when you get the next one, process no more than one per calendar month. There's no rush; you have two years to complete the assignment."

"Seems odd," he said. "Why so long?"

"Like so many things in the lawyering business, it's what the client wants, and he pays the bill."

"Anything else I should know?" Austin asked.

"Regarding payment," she replied: "My client will pay a $25,000 advance, then $25,000 as each parcel is successfully secreted away. You'll receive $5,000 per month for expenses, which you don't have to document, and upon successfully completing the assignment, there will be a $50,000 bonus."

"Generous," Austin said, "in fact more like being dramatically overpaid."

"My client believes it's worth it," C. Monica said, "which brings me to the last but most important rule.

"Rule Seven: Do not call attention to yourself. Do not suddenly develop a noticeably ostentatious lifestyle. For example, don't buy a new car if what you have is sufficient. Don't pay for small items with $100 bills or leave outrageous tips. Don't run up huge buy-everybody-a-drink bar tabs or buy a house full of 70-inch TVs or start putting your nieces and nephews through college."

"Stay off the radar," he said, nodding.

"Exactly. Be mindful of all Rules I've explained to you, but especially Rule Seven."

"They all sound perfectly reasonable to me," Austin said. "I'm in."

"Perfect," C. Monica replied, "welcome to the Seventeen Parcel Project."

After an hour of reading and signing a stack of legally binding agreements, Austin Somerfeld walked out the law office door with a parcel under his arm and a $30,000 check in his pocket.

So far, it had been an excellent day.

CHAPTER 2

What Was Going on in His Head?

The relevant and colorful details about Austin Somerfeld mentioned earlier included being trustworthy, loyal, helpful, thrifty, persistent, self-reliant, and other such Boy-Scout-Law attributes.

He was also invisible.

Nobody noticed him.

Though he was tall, slim, and reasonably good-looking, he had a very familiar face. He reminded people of someone they knew – their banker, their dentist, their ex-husband, or somebody they'd met at a party or bar. He had fluffy sandy hair, no mustache, beard, or even scruff, and usually dressed unremarkably. He could walk through a crowded shopping mall and no one would remember seeing him. They would instead vaguely remember someone else entirely.

He could sit alone at a lunch table in a room full of co-workers and no one would sit with him. Of course, they might notice him if he stood on the table making balloon animals while reciting Annabel Lee, but there was no guarantee. As a result – or perhaps this was the cause – he was very mild-mannered and low-key. He took new developments calmly and rarely got excited or ever panicked about much of anything.

This likely explained why he never had a steady girlfriend. After about the first hour of a date, girls thought he was boring. He didn't join in. He sat on the sidelines and observed but didn't comment. No one knew what was going on in his head and seldom did anyone ask. Very often, his date found an excuse to exit early.

What was going on in his head?

The usual haphazard assortment.

His mind wandered randomly topic to topic, paused occasionally, then skipped ahead or back or somewhere else entirely and meandered on. He could focus intently or not focus at all. Thus, as an activity or occupation, driving fit him perfectly. He could pay attention to the road

7

and traffic, reach a destination safely and on time, and still think about a thousand things along the way.

Today he drove his late-model Ford back to his apartment thinking about his new assignment: The Seventeen Parcel Project. While not as sinister a name as Operation Neptune Spear or The Manhattan Project, it did give a sense of being part of something which mattered to someone. Just who it mattered to was known only as "the client," with no further elaboration, but perhaps this scrap of data would combine with others as time went on and reveal a bigger picture.

The object C. Monica had given him was a black plastic box with no markings save the word "Twelve" written in red letters. It was about the size and shape of a ream of copy machine paper and was sealed shut. It would be easy to hide, and having all parcels the same size made the process even easier.

But just leaving said parcel somewhere seemed insufficient.

It would be best to have safeguards, some expect-the-worst precautions.

Protection from weather, for example, and continued protection if it were hidden for an extended time.

What if an unauthorized somebody accidentally found a parcel after he'd hidden it?

What if an authorized somebody came looking for a parcel at some unknown future date and couldn't find it?

What if ... one thing, and what if ... another thing, and what if ... something else?

He was being substantially overpaid for some reason so he felt obliged to address such what-ifs. To this end, he decided he'd prepare each parcel to survive undamaged for possibly years in any location, he'd leave no evidence behind which led to its untimely discovery, and he'd create a clear path for those who someday would come to find it.

Also – and who would have ever thought he'd have this problem – having money pile up substantially in his currently modest bank account seemed not exactly a staying-off-the-radar thing to do.

These observations of Austin's wandering mind called out for an evening perusing the Knows-all, Tells-all, Solves-all, Internet.

He began by opening three bank accounts: one in Wamego, Kansas, home of the Wizard of Oz Museum, one in Corbin, Kentucky, home of Colonel Sanders' original KFC Cafe, and one in Kitty Hawk, North Carolina, and everyone knows what happened there.

Why these places?

They seemed reasonable at the time.

Each bank wanted documents proving his existence and whereabouts and general worthiness. He located those, scanned copies, and e-mailed them off.

Further thought and research eventually produced online orders for four items:

- Twenty white plastic tubs with clamping, sealable lids 15" x 11" x 3" or about a third again the parcel's dimensions.
- Twenty heavy, plastic, odor-proof bags – like those hikers use to bury food – each big enough to contain a parcel.
- Twenty larger such bags, big enough to contain the white plastic tub.
- Locator beacons to place inside each tub to show its whereabouts as a red dot on a map on his phone. He could turn the beacon on and off remotely if he were within a half-mile of it, and the phone would beep increasingly and the dot blink more rapidly as he drew near.

Nothing in his agreement said he'd be the one coming to *find* these parcels, but sooner or later, *someone* would be coming, and it was good to make the process reasonably easy.

Austin also purchased 20 postage-paid mailing labels which he specified to read *Return if found to C. Monica Stansbury, Esq.,* her law office address, and the warning *Do Not Open*. If someone found a parcel prematurely, this gave him a possible chance to recover it and do the job over.

These supplies arrived within a week and he prepared the first parcel.

He stuck a return-if-found label on the parcel itself, closed it inside a small odor-proof bag, put the bag in a white plastic tub along with a locator beacon, positioned the tub's lid and clamped it shut, inserted the tub in the larger odor-proof bag, and sealed it. It was a bit overdone, perhaps, but who knew how long it would have to last or what external conditions of its ultimate location might beset it.

He activated the locator beacon with his phone, got a satisfying red dot on a map and a beep indicating it was close by, then turned it off.

Parcel Twelve was ready for its hiding place wherever it might be.

The three banks approved his new accounts. Responding to their inquiry about an initial deposit, he sent each $5,000 from his advance, which left them all duly satisfied.

He sent account numbers to C. Monica requesting she deposit expense money in his local bank and split the $25,000 payments a third to each new account. All transaction amounts were thus below IRS reporting mandates.

Next morning, he loaded Parcel Twelve and personal gear, locked his apartment, and drove down the road.

He didn't set a destination on the vehicle's navigation system.

He had no idea where he was going.

CHAPTER 3

He Was Here with No Plan

Austin drove east on I-40 on a windy, overcast May morning. He wasn't driving the package delivery van; this was a personal matter, so he was in his Ford.

The route took him through essentially flat, open country, across occasional rivers, past a few aging billboards advertising goods and services he didn't need, and neither through nor even near any small towns.

He was thinking about carrots roasting in maple syrup.

How long did you roast them?

Did you peel them first?

Did you chop them up or roast them whole?

Was it real maple syrup or something out of a chemistry lab? And how much of it?

It sounded good, maybe with a pork chop and cranberry sauce. Perhaps he would try it someday.

He eventually crossed a long bridge over Lake Eufala, turned northeast on US 69, and reached Muskogee, Oklahoma, in a little over two hours on the road. Clouds had cleared and the wind had settled down. He drove around downtown a short time, then parked in various places and walked about looking for inspiration about hiding places.

Trails in the area seemed primarily for dog-walking.

Not a good choice. People with dogs came at all hours of the day or night. Getting an hour or more alone to dig a hole and bury something might be a problem. Also, dogs were curious and liked to dig, though a dog wouldn't likely smell something sealed in two plastic containers and two layers of odor-proof bags. The same was probably true of coyotes or whatever other wild creatures might be in the area.

There was a cemetery with open space and clumps of trees, but he'd have to be there at night to have time and solitude to do a proper job.

Sleeping a night in a cemetery sounded creepy enough to be worth doing, but he hadn't brought his camping gear. An oversight: he'd remember to include it on future trips.

Campgrounds in remote areas and buildings with expansive wooded grounds offered promise, but they'd also have to be approached at night, which meant hanging around town doing nothing another ten hours. He might become conspicuous, people wondering who he was and what he was up to.

He clearly should have thought about this more; he was here with no plan.

He hadn't even brought a shovel.

Not a good start.

He checked bus stations. Either they didn't have storage lockers, or he didn't notice them. No help there.

Post Office: What if he mailed the parcel to another town, went there and put in a card forwarding the parcel back here, then left a forwarding card here to send it back there?

An amusing idea, but probably not wise. Forwarding had a time limit, like maybe a year or so. Also, workers would soon catch on as the package went back and forth in an endless loop, maybe 60 times a year. What would they do about it? Open it? Throw it away? Put it on a shelf in one place or another and let it sit? Cross that thought off the list, for sure.

It was nearly noon so Austin found a stool at a downtown pub for lunch. Working through burger, fries, and a local tap beer, he struck up conversation with people sitting near him – what to do in town, where to go for dinner, any movie theaters or live music anywhere, and the like. He got lots of suggestions.

"Are you visiting friends here?" one fellow asked.

"No," Austin replied, "just passing through town."

"Well," the fellow went on, "35,000 or so of us Okies from Muskogee live here. We have museums for Native American history and Oklahoma music, and there's an old submarine in a War Memorial Park you can check out. Enough to keep you busy a few hours."

He eventually asked about pawn shops.

"Are you selling guns?" one asked.

"Not guns; just an old guitar I never learned to play."

"If you had guns, I might be interested."

"You could try Double D," another man said. "I bought some tools there once. It worked out pretty well."

"I originally bought the guitar at a pawn shop," Austin went on. "Turns out I didn't have a talent for it. Too many things to be doing at once, and then there's the whole business of singing whatever song you're trying to play, remembering the notes and the words, it just didn't work."

"I know what you mean," the fellow said. "I tried welding once but just made a mess of it. It burned me pretty bad and set my garage on fire. Not my best idea."

"Sounds scary," Austin said. "I suppose the guitar is about practice and dedication to learning. I guess I didn't have it."

Nor did he have a guitar.

So, after lunch and further good-natured conversation, he went to Double D Pawn and Gun Shop just a few minutes away. A friendly, middle-aged man in a blue striped shirt greeted him.

"What can I help you with?"

"Could I leave a package here and pick it up at some later date?"

"Yes, you can, but how much later?"

"I don't know; it could be years."

"Years ... possibly a problem there. How big a package?"

"I'll get it," Austin said, "just a minute."

He brought the parcel in its elaborate wrappings and set it on the counter.

"Oh, about the size of a good socket wrench kit," the man said. "It won't be a problem. Of course, a full drum set or a room full of electronics equipment would be a different story. But I'll have to charge you something."

"Would $200 work?"

"It would, and maybe another hundred or two when you pick it up, depending on how long it's been here."

Austin nodded in reply. The man recorded the item, gave him a claim ticket, and accepted $200 cash in twenties.

"Thanks for your business," he said and disappeared into the back room carrying Parcel Twelve in its tub.

Outside, Austin checked the beacon locator map on his phone. There it was, a red dot blinking in Muskogee. He used the phone to turn the beacon off so its batteries wouldn't drain, then headed back the 140 miles to his apartment in Oklahoma City.

13

One day's work for $25,000, he thought; nice work if you can get it. But it seemed so far afield from a regular rate of pay it was making him suspicious.

Was this part of some larger and darker plot in which he was the fall guy?

Was he followed here?

Might Parcel Twelve possibly be stolen from the pawnshop, and he be held responsible?

What if it were full of cash or diamonds or military secrets?

What if ... what if he was just being paranoid?

"Oh, you're just fussing," he could hear his mom saying. "Find something else to think about."

Very well, he concluded; he would wait and see.

Meanwhile, he followed the Rules. Once home, he wrote the required letter to the law office (Rule Four), included the claim ticket and the pawn shop's GPS location, which he'd gotten from his phone, made copies of everything for himself, then mailed the letter. It had "12" written on the outside as directed.

He followed up with an e-mail (Rule Five) specifying his apartment address for C. Monica to send him the next parcel.

FedEx brought it two days later: same size, same description.

Welcome Parcel Three.

CHAPTER 4

A Time to Set Ideas Loose

Austin did his homework this time before blasting cluelessly down the road. According to the Rules, he couldn't stash further parcels in Oklahoma so he looked north into Kansas and Nebraska for a peaceful, out-of-the-way location. He settled on Chautauqua Park Campground in Beatrice, Nebraska. It seemed suitably quiet and woodsy in its picture on the Internet.

So, on a sunny afternoon in early June, he loaded camp gear and folding shovel into his Ford, put Parcel Three in the front passenger seat footwell and departed about noon. It was just under 400 miles north to Wichita, then Salina, then on narrower roads past a few smaller towns into Nebraska. He planned to arrive early evening, near dark.

Somewhere that afternoon, in the stretch of flat, often-featureless countryside, he saw a billboard:

Admit it

You're Curious

Visit the Spam Museum

Well, he *hadn't* been curious, but suddenly now he was. Where was the Spam Museum anyway? Someplace in Minnesota? Why would it have a billboard in Kansas? Why not? Wall Drug signs were everywhere.

Perhaps he should keep driving until he found this museum, whatever it was. He could probably get a Spam T-shirt there, or a Spam ballcap, or any of a hundred other must-have Spam things. Perhaps tomorrow he should have Spam for breakfast.

Really curious now, he pulled to the roadside to find out how far away it was. Answer: another 400 miles. It didn't matter how far away, he'd told C. Monica, and it was tempting ... but not today.

And so went the lesson in how advertising works, he thought, amused.

His steady pace brought him to the campground just after six o'clock. He registered for a site near the woods, then put up his Big Agnes one-person tent such a masterpiece of engineering it weighed only two pounds.

Later he went to town to look around, have dinner, and spend a couple of hours at a bar. He'd dressed differently this time, in a different shirt and jeans and sneakers but still totally anonymous and unrememberable. He wore a random baseball cap from the dozen or so on his closet shelf.

"How is this town's name pronounced?" he asked the bartender. "I've heard it a couple of different ways."

"It's not how you'd think, like the girl's name," the bartender answered. "That's BE-a-tris. The town was named for a girl, the daughter of one of the founders, but she pronounced it Be-AT-ris, like in th$^\theta$ee-AT-ric, to be different. You might say she was being th$^\theta$ee-AT-ri-cal."

"I would never have figured that out," Austin said. "Thanks for today's bit of history."

"Can I get you something?"

"You have a bottle of Bushmill's Black Bush hiding back there. I'll have a double shot, neat, please."

He sipped at his whiskey and resumed being invisible. He knew the longer he sat there, the more invisible he would become, almost becoming part of the furniture.

He would wear something equally anonymous on future stops and order a different drink. For example, bartenders would remember if he always ordered a Mai Tai. It was about not leaving a recognizable pattern behind if anyone happened to be paying attention. More than likely, nobody was.

He could accomplish the same thing asleep in his tent, but no one served drinks there.

Back at the campsite about ten o'clock, he carried gear from the car in his backpack, another wonder of design, along with Parcel Three suited up in its Coat of Many Colors as he termed its various layers of protection. Finally, after arranging the tent and settling in, he drifted off to sleep.

His phone alarm buzzed at three in the morning. The night had a dim glow of moonlight and no lights or sounds came from the few tents and camper vehicles around him. He gathered up the parcel and other gear, crawled out of the tent, and vanished silently into the woods.

He selected a spot about 300 feet away. It was slightly open, had only a bit of leafy ground cover, and did not appear full of tangled roots. He cleared the leaves and spread a tarp on the ground, then quietly dug a hole about three feet deep, shoveling removed dirt onto the tarp.

About the time he'd nearly finished an owl chose the moment to screech loudly. Austin froze. Screech owls made their shrieking sound to intimidate prey, trying to make them dart from one hiding place to perhaps a better one, intending to dive and catch them as they ran.

Was the owl screeching at Austin, annoyed at him for chasing small creatures away with his digging?

More to the point, would the loud noise awaken campers and bring them out to look around?

Austin laid down on the ground and remained motionless. The owl screeched again; no one stirred in the campground. Austin put the packaged parcel at the bottom of the hole, tested the locator beacon, then gently filled the void with dirt from the tarp. He restored and arranged the leaves and produced a scene looking much as he'd found it, then stealthily returned to his tent.

In the morning, he lay just listening. People around him made wake-up sounds, breakfast sounds, and packing-to-leave sounds. They seemed hopeful about what the new day might bring and soon many were gone.

No one talked about hearing noises in the night.

No one wondered who the occupant of the solitary tent might be.

No one had noticed him at all.

Austin pondered the once-a-month Rule as he lay there. If he had all 17 parcels, he could get this project done in two or three weeks in one long, intense road trip. Instead, Rule Six meant many trips, longer each time to accomplish the same thing.

Maybe he should talk to C. Monica about it.

But then again, maybe not.

She would surely tell him the client made the Rules, not she, and Austin should just get used to it. After all, she was paying him more than enough for the job, however seemingly inconvenient it might be.

Best to save the embarrassment, he concluded, and follow the Rules, which is what he'd agreed to do in the first place.

So, this fine morning it was back on the road, back to a day of looking straight ahead and occasionally to the side as thoughts bounced around his head randomly one against another, leading to who knows what, if anything. In Austin's experience, this was the best use of his time while driving.

Even in a vehicle that manages its speed, headlight beams, and windshield wipers, and that beeps a warning when you get too close to something in a parking lot or dense traffic, and that robotically stays in its lane matching speed with the vehicle ahead while maintaining properly safe intervening distance, and that automatically calculates and gives insistent navigation directions, and that monitors on-going mechanical performance and lets you know if anything is amiss ... even with the vehicle doing all these things on its own, driving is a busy thing.

Stay between the lines and don't hit anything is an excellent general plan, but the innocuous and generic landscape accompanying most roadways (some would call it peaceful) is often interrupted by narrow and restricted lanes from construction which goes on for miles, or accidents causing traffic to slow down, stop altogether, then creep ahead, condensing and expanding like an accordion, or curious messages written by finger on dirty cars and tractor-trailer rear doors, or clever vanity plates like B0NLY1 or HIHOAG, or multiple billboards promising food and sleep and gas and entertainment just a few miles ahead, not to mention accident and personal injury lawyers.

Or sometimes, if good fortune is indeed in a pleasant mood, there comes a sudden vast emptiness stretching in all directions as if the world has abruptly gone silent with only the scenic vista as an interlude.

In short: there are distractions, some pleasing, some not.

Today, several thoughts were rolling around Austin's mind.

What was he doing here?

Of what grand scheme had he become a part?

He was carrying something to conceal in distant places and being paid handsomely to do it.

Why? It sounded like he'd been enlisted as a drug mule, except he got to choose the destination, and there was no one to meet him for delivery.

C. Monica had assured him the project involved nothing stolen or illegal, yet the puzzle remained: what was involved?

"You're still fussing," he heard his mom say.

C. Monica said he didn't need to know, and he'd accepted and signed an agreement saying so, but it was still a curious line of thought to drift about his head with other random things.

He was back in Oklahoma City by late afternoon. He wrote the attorney letter telling of the current resting place of Parcel Three, then took his thoughts a step further.

It would be another month before he could deal with whichever parcel came next. Perhaps he should plan, or even schedule, remaining stops instead of just meandering about the countryside.

He knew how many parcels there were.

He knew the Rules.

Maybe he should just get to work.

An evening on the computer produced a map with a grand spiraling line going west into Oregon, south through California, east through Texas and Georgia, and eventually north through the Carolinas, Maryland, and Maine. It was 7,500 miles if done all at once. One stop a month would be several times that.

What does it matter, he thought; it's a dream road trip with all expenses paid.

It didn't matter how far anything was.

It was time to quit complaining and enjoy the ride.

CHAPTER 5

He Apologized to No One

Xander Moorhouse was a quiet man, getting on in years, who went about his business not attracting headlines. He worked from the study in his spacious Oklahoma City home expertly using the Internet and a network of brokers around the US to manage a portfolio of investments worth, at the moment, $957 million. He wasn't on anyone's list of wealthiest people, and though Forbes Magazine had inquired about an interview, Moorhouse had declined.

He was not the stereotype image of a powerful billionaire tycoon. He was short, a bit portly, and bushy – bushy white hair, bushy white eyebrows, and a bushy white mustache. His eyes were severe and penetrating behind glasses with thick black frames.

He wore dress pants and shined shoes, a crisp white shirt, and a colorful necktie every day for work (including weekends), even in his own home office. He frequently smoked cigars, for which he apologized to no one, and kept a bottle of $65 bourbon and a heavy sculpted rocks glass never far out of reach. Had his picture appeared in a financial magazine with his customary disinterested, dismissive, yet fiercely intent expression, readers might have identified him as somewhere between Dr. Strangelove harboring some dark secret and Colonel Sanders selling chicken.

Though he often went to local and out-of-town restaurants, at home he prepared his meals from groceries he ordered on the Internet. Not wanting to be bothered with it some days, he had an Uber driver bring him his one true favorite: a Jersey Mike's #13 sub.

He'd been a lawyer in his day, not a personal injury lawyer, bankruptcy lawyer, corporate lawyer, family practice lawyer, or even a criminal lawyer, but a whatever-walks-in-the-door lawyer.

He represented anyone.

Most paid his rate of $450 an hour; some paid nothing at all. Successfully representing a client in a courtroom, he quickly learned, or negotiating a satisfactory settlement was where the big money was.

Success came to him many more times than not, which attracted increasing numbers of big-ticket cases, and he amassed a sizable fortune over the years. He invested successfully and steadily turned his fortune into great wealth.

He had interests beyond his investment portfolio but they specifically did not include expensive cars, boats, airplanes, motorcycles, or anything similarly flamboyant requiring storage space and maintenance. It was just showing off, in his opinion. Instead, he sought rare items of the day's culture that he could buy anonymously at online auctions and put away until someone else wanted them at a higher price.

Xander's wife had been a shining bright spot in his early life and the source of many happy memories. More and more, however, he'd become so occupied with his law practice and investments his attention was elsewhere. They'd had three children over five years, and so it eventually transpired she spent her time tending children, and he went to work.

A failed respiratory system took her life when the children were teens. Xander was attentive to her during her illness, arranging home care and sitting by her bedside hour after hour, and making what remained of her life as comfortable as he could. Her death was a tragedy for them all, but the children took care of themselves after that, and Moorhouse returned to his work.

He became distant and absorbed.

No one – not he, not the children – did anything about it.

No one knew how.

He was not a lavish spender. He provided more than adequately for the children and the household, but otherwise, now 64 years old and no longer practicing law, he sat in his study engrossed with making new asset acquisitions.

His holdings had grown to be appropriately diverse: upscale office buildings, sprawling commercial properties, an impressive roster of blue-chip stocks, nose-bleed expensive high-rise apartments, 250,000 acres of Oklahoma bare land, a National League hockey team, a dozen bank accounts with substantial balances, movie rights to three brilliant new novels, and private vaults in five unknown locations around the US containing millions in raw cash. He'd made himself massively rich yet preferred nobody noticed.

The hockey team had been a diversion. It was losing money when Moorhouse bought it several years before and continued to do so season after season. He was setting up to sell it at a spectacular loss. The resulting negative publicity would discourage undue interest in his steady string of dramatic successes.

In fact, after his lifetime of continuous acquisition, Moorhouse was now selling everything. Quietly and methodically over the past several years, he'd been unloading properties at huge profits, liquidating stocks bought ages ago at up to 30 times what he paid, closing US bank accounts, and slowly transferring proceeds to investment accounts he'd opened in Singapore.

He'd made excellent progress on this campaign so far. He figured that all trace of Xander Moorhouse would be gone from the US financial scene in a couple more years. And, because of more favorable offshore banking laws, no one could claim his wealth or even know its value.

This dramatic change in strategy was all because of the children, now grown and with lives of their own. Though they'd shown much intelligence and promise as youngsters, they now, in his estimation, seemed content with mediocrity. He saw them as if from afar and was disappointed. He didn't know and hadn't learned how to help them. He wasn't sure they wanted help, especially from him.

The problem he saw coming was they stood to inherit his fortune when he died. It was only proper to leave it to them – doing otherwise would be thoughtless and cruel – but he feared they would squander it foolishly, destroying their own lives and everything he'd built.

The financial portfolio he'd constructed was complex and required close attention. He could keep details in his head of dozens of things going on today, another dozen tomorrow, and more happening a month from now. The children might have the ability between the three of them to do this, but likely not the interest.

Caroline was the eldest. Now 34, a curly-haired blonde of medium height and slight build, she had a weary disposition and always seemed dissatisfied about something. She'd married a man named Griffith and had two children: Rory Michael Griffith, now age eight, and Sandra Ellen Griffith, age six. Unfortunately, her husband had abruptly left, and a second husband, whose name she never adopted, later did the same, leaving her with a perhaps justifiable sour attitude and two children to raise on her own.

She'd developed no particular skills. She had almost no self-esteem or self-respect and constantly dressed like a street urchin. Her typical day's outfit from her nearly empty closet was a ragged T-shirt, an occasional sweatshirt with an OKC Thunder logo, jeans with large holes, and a pair of worn-out sneakers. She often wore the same clothes days at a time.

She regularly complained to her younger brother and her little sister – when she would listen – about needing more money to exist. Yes, dad still gave them each $5,000 a month for living expenses and had paid off mortgages on their homes, but she needed more merely to break even. She seemed stuck in her helplessness and brooded about her dull, dead-end life.

But she did an excellent job of being a mom. She provided for her kids as well as she was able and helped them through their problems growing up. They loved and were respectful to her, and having them around afforded what little happiness existed in her life.

David was 32. He was tall, stout, and already balding with faint wisps of fly-away brown hair. He had a pleasant personality, got along with nearly everyone, but lacked ambition or imagination. He could have been inventive and successful but instead turned out to be someone who would go to Baskin Robbins and order a vanilla cone.

He bumbled his way through life, not striving for greatness, or even competence in much of anything. On rare occasions when this began to trouble him, rather than pursue some positive self-improvement plan he'd get hold of a supply of weed and spend a day or two getting stoned. Doing this at home was one thing; driving around town believing he was invincible was quite another.

David sometimes thought he should break free of his deepening rut and do something significant like restoring an old car, running for mayor, or climbing Mt. Kilimanjaro. But it was all too much bother. He was sure to lose interest before long and end up with an abandoned old car and its parts, campaign leaflets and signs, or expensive hiking gear littering the garage.

He'd failed and been let go from a long list of jobs and was barely hanging onto the one he had now. He could do the work assigned to him when he showed up and could focus.

In his defense, David was devoted to his wife, Becky, and made every effort to help her and be attentive to her needs. The same age as he, Becky had been in a disastrous car accident five years before which she'd caused, unfortunately, by talking distracted on her phone. Her vehicle automatically called 911 and a fire department emergency crew arrived within minutes to extract her from the tangled wreck. It was heartbreaking for both David and Becky to learn she'd never walk again and, for the foreseeable future, would be confined to a wheelchair.

She was a lovely, agreeable woman, brilliant, and nearly always cheerful. Though officially disabled, she got around the house and town ably maneuvering her wheelchair and car without assistance.

David and Becky did everything together and about a year ago had developed an abiding common interest: playing Monopoly. He'd gotten out the game one evening for them to play just for something to do together.

It was fun.

They both loved it.

Since then, they'd set up the board several evenings a week to play and had even collected different versions of the game – they had a stack of 37 of them in the guest room.

Juliana was the exception. At 29, she was quick and bright and, on her own, had opened five hugely successful fitness studios in Oklahoma City. She worked and worked out in one or more of them nearly every week and, as a result, definitely looked the part. She was tall, thin, muscular, and maintained an enviable level of fitness. She was also beautiful: long, straight brown hair, striking facial features, an ever-present smile, and to make it clear to all she was a serious businesswoman, almost always wore a skirt, coordinated blouse and blazer, and shoes a grade above sensible.

She was unmarried. With her mother and Caroline's two husbands gone, she shied away from such attachment. But she attracted a seemingly endless parade of fit, good-looking males among members and personal trainers in her studios.

Unlike her siblings, she was active in the community. She'd served on museum boards, city planning commissions, and business association committees and occasionally carried petitions door-to-door for signature.

She lived in a modest residence, drove an unpretentious car, and had no elaborate collections of art, jewelry, or expensive wines. She worked to live and lived to work. It paid the bills and was what she knew how to do.

She still received the $5,000 a month like the others and put it toward her businesses. But though she appreciated her father's monthly check, she vaguely disliked him for growing so distant after their mother passed away.

She seldom asked his advice or support, yet somehow secretly desired it. She would welcome a long conversation with him about business success and an opportunity for the two of them to share stories about what they each did well. But she never asked, nor did he.

Meanwhile, dad – Xander Moorhouse, at home in his study – was placing stacks of documents and paper-clipped bundles of clippings and receipts into three more plastic boxes: Parcel Five, Parcel Seven, and Parcel Eleven. A courier would pick them up tomorrow morning and deliver them to the law office of C. Monica Stansbury, Esq. He'd sent her most of the 17 parcels now; there were only a few yet to fill.

The young man she'd chosen to go about the country hiding them had asked few questions about such a puzzling assignment. He'd accepted the job and was doing it.

It was an excellent start.

But he would get to wondering about it over time: who, and what, and why. Moorhouse was interested to learn where such idle ponderings might lead.

Rules: Completing the task without breaking any would greatly benefit him.

Consequences: Breaking Rules, any of them, would bring him and everyone else problems.

CHAPTER 6

I Am Not Worthy

Austin drove 13 hours nonstop through rain and gusting wind to reach the Rapid City, South Dakota, bus station before it closed at 6:00 PM. He arrived in time, and as he'd hoped, it had storage lockers. There was no sign specifying time limits for using them but, just to be sure, he asked around for anyone's remembrance of a general locker cleanout.

"Someone left something smelly in one a year or so back," one employee told him. "They opened it and tossed the stuff away, but it's the only time I can remember." Moderately reassured, he placed Parcel Seven inside a locker and pocketed the key.

He chose a place for dinner and ordered a steak, a salad, and a martini. The drink soon arrived, and he noticed the mid-50s man in a gray trilby hat sitting two seats down had ordered a martini as well. The bartender was preparing it with gin, as Austin thought it should be, but was using generic gin from the rail.

"Have you ever tried Bombay Sapphire or a Navy strength gin?" Austin asked the man.

A wistful look passed over his face. "Oh, no, I am not worthy," he said with a bit of a smile.

"Then allow me," Austin said and turned to the bartender, "please change this gentleman's order. Make it with Bombay Sapphire Gin, just a faint whisper of dry Vermouth, and either one or three olives. Put it on my tab. Oh, and very important: stirred, not shaken."

"I prefer onions, actually," the man said.

"Then make him a Gibson, same ingredients, no olives."

"Thank you very much, my friend; this will be a pleasant treat. What is Navy strength, by the way?"

"In the 18th century, the British Navy stored their allotment of gin next to the gunpowder. They made sure the gin was at least 57% alcohol so gunpowder would still ignite if someone spilled gin into it."

26

"You suppose they could have stored it somewhere else?" the man asked, then added, "That much alcohol strikes me as rather strong."

"It is," Austin replied. "More than one drink leaves my head decidedly buzzed."

"Oh, and you also said 'one olive or three,' why not two?"

"In certain establishments during Prohibition, if a bartender served your drink with two olives it was a warning someone meant you harm. It was a sign to drink up and take off."

"Definitely a new one on me," the man said, "but I must be safe if I'm asking for onions."

"I think then you get a pass," said Austin.

"You're just a young man. How did you become so knowledgeable about this sophisticated cocktail at such an early age?"

"Tending bar was one of my jobs out of high school. It was in an upscale place and I met martini snobs, some who said gin made the only authentic martini, others who insisted on vodka. I soon became a snob as well, of the gin variety, preferably heavy on juniper."

"I wholeheartedly agree," the man said. "In fact, among us gin snobs, most agree concoctions like the Lemon Drop Martini, the Chocolate Martini, or the Coconut Cream Pie Martini – essentially just pouring anything into a cocktail glass and calling it a martini – are a clear indication of civilization's imminent decline."

Austin nodded his agreement.

The drinks came, they expressed their approvals, then continued their conversation for another hour.

Austin had worn one of his baseball caps through the day but removed it when his food arrived. It was what his mother taught him, and even though she wasn't anywhere nearby he still did what she said out of respect for her and good manners. The cap had a Pennzoil logo which wouldn't identify him to any particular location. He was just a guy passing through looking for a steak, a salad, and a well-made martini.

Move along, folks; nothing to see here.

Rain had ended hours before, so he went to the local KOA to camp for the night. He had enough cash for a $100 motel room, of course, but an anonymous tent was the stay-off-the-radar choice, at least in decent weather.

He slept comfortably through the night. No one had noisy campfire parties in his vicinity, no police cars pulled up with lights flashing to search vehicles or take anyone in for "questioning," no wildlife invaded

27

his tent. It was as pleasant as any motel room, just no morning shower or complimentary breakfast.

Austin dreamed he was chauffeuring Carrie Fisher cross-country to a Star Wars movie marathon in Los Angeles. She'd died years before but materialized as a ghostly apparition in the back seat of a white limousine Austin was driving. She said little but ate steadily from a bag of Snickers bars while she watched *The Blues Brothers* movie on her phone.

Austin drove in silence and watched the road, stopping only for gas and occasional sleep during which the apparition faded away, then returned. Arriving in LA, the ghostly figure pleasantly said "Thank you," slowly dematerialized and left a $20,000 tip, which also soon disappeared.

He drove southwest next morning instead of heading directly home. Winding mountain roads took him 26 miles to Mt. Rushmore National Memorial. Displays at its Visitor Center showed photographs of progress on the massive sculpture from the time work began in 1927, explaining the stone-working techniques of the day. He found information regarding the dispute between the Lakota Sioux and the US Government over who in fact owned the land, as well as the tedious, on-going debate about whether such work was appropriate in nature.

Sculptor Gutzon Borglum chose the four US Presidents represented. Faces are 60 feet tall but were initially intended to be figures shown from the waist up. Upon entering World War II, the US ran out of money for the project and declared it finished in 1941.

Austin then drove to Crazy Horse Monument nearby, a work in progress begun in 1948. Envisioned as a 606-foot-tall carving of a warrior on horseback, only the warrior's head was identifiable so far. This massive carving undertaken by the Lakota Sioux tribe would represent their role and presence in the area. The finished work would be genuinely majestic, as shown by Visitor Center models, but completion might be half a century away.

He then turned south and headed into Nebraska and Kansas for the journey home. He moved steadily along the occasionally frantic, but more often monotonous highway wondering about something he'd wondered about before: what was actually in the parcels. So far, those he'd handled were not empty; they weighed different amounts. One made slapping sounds when he shook it like it was only partly full. Another was slightly bulging and made no sound at all.

As clues went, it wasn't much to go on. Maybe some future parcel would be a rattler, sounding like it was full of marbles, or a rustler like it contained Christmas socks wrapped in tissue paper. Such additional clues would also be essentially meaningless and lead to no conclusions at all.

But it didn't matter.

Sometime long after he'd completed the Seventeen Parcel Project there would come a day when all would be revealed.

Perhaps he'd have a chance to learn what those revelations were.

Aside from such idle curiosity, he had no desire to open them. After all, he delivered packages all day at his job and didn't know or care what was in them. Why should he be interested now? If it wasn't for Rule One – do not open them, not ever – it might never have occurred to him to wonder.

He turned east for a 50-mile side trip to Lincoln, Nebraska. He paid $15 admission to visit the Museum of American Speed, a 150,000 square foot building displaying a continuous chronology of beautifully designed racing cars and powerful engines. It was three floors jammed with dragsters, motors, and other speed equipment, with historical and technological features explained by posted signs.

Austin spent three hours roaming the informative displays. He had no particular interest in racing but this was a fascinating collection of products of human ingenuity. Besides, it was something different to see and a minor detour from the most efficient way home.

The USA was full of such "points of interest."

Why just drive without going to see them?

He got gas in Lincoln and used his phone to check his three new account balances. The first two payments were there, evenly distributed as requested.

C. Monica was also following the Rules.

It was the thing to do.

CHAPTER 7

How Did I Get Here?

Police arrested David Moorhouse.

Again.

His father had bailed him out and lawyered him up often during his youth, yet David took from it no lasting lessons learned. Dad got him out; all was good. Arrests happened less frequently now but still often enough for the desk sergeant to say: "Good evening, Mr. Moorhouse" when an officer brought David in.

This time he'd been driving high on weed and had stopped at a traffic light. Three hours later, he was still idling at the same intersection, wholly captivated by the bright colors of changing lights. Motorists drove around him, and eventually, one called police.

"They're so ROUND," he said to the officer who tapped on his window and finally got his attention. "They're *round*," he went on, "and big and so many bright colors. I can't decide which one I like best. The yellow one? Maybe the green. No, it has to be the red one. I should watch them again to make sure."

Police escorted him to jail, had his car towed, and next morning he awoke feeling hungry, a bit spaced, and wondering where he was. The place looked familiar, he thought, but he was tired and went back to sleep until an officer banged on his cell door.

"Someone's here to see you," the officer said. It was Juliana. She'd been here to do this before.

"Becky called me when you didn't come home," she said. "You remember Becky, your wife, don't you? County Jail was the first place she checked to find you."

"What happened?" he asked. "How did I get here?"

"The usual," she answered. "You got yourself high and couldn't make it home. Something about staring at street lights for several hours, the officer said."

"Oh, I know," David said, "I'm in jail."

"You're such a genius."

"Can you get me out?"

"I paid your fine," Juliana replied. "We can leave now unless you'd rather stay a few days. Accommodations here don't look very comfortable in my seldom asked for but never humble opinion."

"Where's my car?"

"In the tow lot. Leave it there until you're thinking more clearly. Let's go get you something to eat; breakfast should help."

David gradually came around during his plateful of pancakes. His father had made the police-station trip to retrieve him in years past but at one point had said: "You're an adult; solve your own problems." Since then, he'd sought help from Juliana, the only one of them who had extra money.

Was there such a thing as extra money? he idly wondered, like, money you didn't need?

If so, he'd never experienced it.

But ... his thoughts continued, it would be an outstanding experience.

"Thanks for coming to get me," he said.

"You're welcome," Juliana replied, "again."

"Again. Yeah, I know, sorry about that. I was bummed over something last night, but now I can't remember what. Well, looking on the bright side, some part of the experience worked out. By the way, I think dad is up to something,"

"What makes you think so?"

"He's always busy in his study with the door pushed nearly closed when I've gone there."

"You know he won't loan you any more money," Juliana replied. "Why go there?"

"I wanted something from my room. He still keeps our rooms the same as when we lived there, as if we're all coming home someday to be a big happy family."

"Like we seldom ever were, but it's sweet of him to be so respectful. Caroline tells me most of mom's things are still there as well, just as she left them, except her jewelry which is missing. Dad wouldn't have sold it; he must have put in some safer place."

"Also," David went on as if he hadn't heard, "there's a courier who comes by to pick up packages. Delivers them to some lawyer downtown. I've seen it happen a couple of times."

"And you followed the courier like some amateur Philip Marlowe out to discover one of dad's deep, dark secrets," Juliana said. "It's interesting, maybe, but more likely just dad being dad. He's this grand, international tycoon, or so he likes to think, so does lots of business deals, which usually involves a lawyer."

"How old is he now?" David asked.

"Mid-sixties, I think, but if you're counting on him to die and leave us everything anytime soon, don't get your hopes up. He's as healthy as can be, and from what you say, apparently busy and not the least bored."

David looked dejected. "It was just a thought. I don't wish him harm or anything. I could just use a million or two."

"The problem with such thinking," Juliana said, rolling her eyes, "is you'd just fritter it away on useless, ill-advised, very bad, not to mention borderline stupid ideas. It would quickly be gone, you'd wonder where it all went, and you'd again be saying, 'I could just use a million or two.'

"Get a job. Show up for work. Do something useful. Live long and prosper."

"I have a job," he replied, "just not a very good one. I've had many jobs, actually, but most haven't lasted very long. You're right; it's the showing up and being useful part, things I've never been good at. I get bored easily and can't stick to things."

"A lot of life is boring," Juliana replied. "I do the same things over and over again every month for my businesses. It's boring, but it brings in money, keeps the companies running, and provides services to help people. According to what little I know about dad, those things are what matters.

"So, big bozo brother," she went on, "here's unsolicited advice I'm sure you don't want to hear: don't be such a whiner. Do something with your life instead of just existing. Be good to Becky; she has more sense than you do."

They left the restaurant and she took David home. She'd pay his towing bill, she told him, and have the car delivered.

"And stay home," Juliana said in parting, "don't drive anywhere."

Meanwhile, Xander Moorhouse was across town in his study, checking bids he'd recently made on collectible items. One was a 1985 Roosevelt dime with die-stamping errors for which the owner was asking $5,000. Xander had the top bid so far at $3,758, with two days remaining on the auction.

If he won it, he'd receive the item by mail soon after, then drive it to the bank to store in a safe deposit box with other such purchases. He didn't put things in albums and leave them on display around the house. He kept them safely stored away to offer for sale someday when their value substantially increased.

If he ever needed money.

Which was unlikely.

This thought pleased his seldom-used sense of humor, and he laughed.

He also checked Sotheby's art auction. Several American artist paintings of broker and stock exchange scenes fascinated him, most in the $20,000 range. He'd purchased two so far and was thinking of getting another. These would go into local storage where he kept valuables he had no place for in the house.

He didn't get involved with works by big-name artists, like Van Gogh paintings selling for more than $80 million. He thought bidding on such items at such a price was showing off and he didn't want the publicity.

Also, owning one would be too much trouble. He couldn't just hang it in the living room or hallway. It would need care, protection, and security; he'd have to loan it to some museum. What was the point? They'd want to put his name on it: "from the collection of Xander Moorhouse" or some such attribution. He didn't want the attention. Besides, he'd prefer to buy many things at reasonable prices than spend a fortune on just one.

An exception to these guidelines was the Honus Wagner card, the most sought-after and thus most expensive baseball card of all. Years ago, he'd bid on one of 50 such cards in existence but stopped when the price went beyond $1 million. A million was a significant percentage of his portfolio back then and became a sort of threshold to him for seemingly frivolous purchases. Said threshold increased as years went on but so had the price of Honus Wagner. One recently sold for more than $6 million, so it was still beyond what Xander was willing to pay, especially for a small piece of cardboard destined to spend its days locked away in a bank vault.

Thus, he was content to buy a coin, stamp, or painting a few times a year to add to his collections. He never documented these acquisitions. In fact, he'd lost all track of how extensive his collections were, but they were safely tucked away one place or another and he could find them if the need arose.

These details out of the way, he began work on a situation that had turned into a problem by the mere passage of time.

His private vaults anonymously located around the US contained about $45 million in actual paper currency, accumulated and stored there in a time when having lots of cash didn't cause suspicion. He couldn't sell and transfer it like the rest of his assets; it all had to be moved physically somewhere, most likely to a bank, which outwardly took on the distinct appearance of laundering money.

He briefly considered starting a new construction project and paying the contractors in cash, but there were many associated problems. Besides being a bit awkward and gangsterish, it would take a minimum of two years even to get a building designed and obtain necessary permits. Then it would need his supervision through the building process and, after that, would require high-value tenants, which should be signed up before work began. He judged it way too demanding at this stage and decided against it.

Buying an existing property like a hotel or apartment building was counter-productive. He was getting rid of things, not adding them.

Giving it to the children was most certainly out. Caroline's and David's lives were steadily going nowhere, at least from his point of view. Just think how they could destroy themselves with too much money. There was hope for Juliana, but he couldn't give her something and not the others. Besides, it wouldn't solve the problem – then they'd have to deal with millions in cash with far fewer resources to do so.

Boxing it up and shipping it somewhere was a terrible plan, especially if the destination was out of the country. How do you explain a Charmin box full of cash – or a dozen of them – to airport security, or anyone? No foreign bank would want it. They preferred a simple wire transfer showing up as a number on a screen.

He thought about it most of the morning and gradually crafted a strategy.

He phoned a banker in each city where vaults were located and explained he'd be having a substantial amount of cash physically delivered to them for processing. They asked how much money, paused briefly in momentary surprise when he told them, then informed him of paperwork he should send them to initiate their management-of-cash procedures and to prevent its seizure by the IRS.

He prepared requested documents and e-mailed them to the individual banks, then arranged for armored car services to go to each

34

vault, pack up its contents, and deliver it safely to said banks.

Each could then process the cash, determine it wasn't counterfeit or stolen in some documented robbery, verify he had no terrorist or drug-cartel ties, charge some exorbitant handling fee, and finally notify him of the result.

Banks surmised it would take two or three weeks, after which he could wire final amounts to brokers in Singapore where they'd appear as desired, a number on a screen.

CHAPTER 8

The Road Has Answers

Austin was back underway in early August. He'd hidden parcels so far in May, June, and July; now he was on his way with Parcel Ten to Billings, Montana.

Billings was a two-day drive from Oklahoma City. Miles passed, then more miles. Hot, sunny weather continued without relief as he sped northward through Kansas and Colorado. His mind wandered, and he began to ponder an enduring road trip mystery.

Where was E?

A dashboard gauge said E was 139 miles away. So if he drove 139 miles, would he be in E, or was 139 just a guess, and he wouldn't be anywhere at all?

But the mystery was more puzzling. If he turned left or right or completely around, E would still be 139 miles away but in another direction. He would always be getting closer no matter which way he went.

Did E move around? Was it even a real place? Did E somehow surround him, and the 139 miles was to the edge? Was he driving out of it instead of toward it?

That would explain a few things, but he'd never been to E, so didn't know.

Even more perplexing, he also knew once he filled up with gas, E would be farther away but still the same distance whichever direction he chose.

Maybe E was some elusive place he was never supposed to find, like Shangri-La or the Lost City of Gold. Maybe E was a mystical dimension where, if he ever did get there, he'd be in a completely new world of strange goings-on.

Someday, Austin thought, he would keep driving until the gauge said 0 miles to E and see what was there. Maybe something. Maybe nothing. Maybe someday.

He stopped late afternoon in Cheyenne, Wyoming.

He'd chosen this stop specifically to spend time searching out Cheyenne Big Boots. These were 25 eight-foot-tall cowboy boots located on the grounds of parks or buildings around the city, and each was painted with colorful Wyoming scenes by local artists.

He found five downtown at Cheyenne Depot Plaza, including Big Boots named "Governors of Wyoming," "Don't Feed the Animals," and "Where the Deer and the Antelope Play." Then he sought out others farther out of town and located "Library Boot" (showing city libraries against a background bookshelf of literary classics), "8 Seconds – Steps to the Big Time" (painted with a progression of bull-riding scenes), and "Gambler's Boot" (featuring a gambler's vest with pockets containing cards, a pocket watch, and a silver dagger). He found 13 of the Big Boots in a few hours.

It was near dark when he set up his tent in nearby Curt Gowdy State Park. The 3,400-acre park offered a richly varied landscape, an extensive trail system, and three huge, rocky reservoirs for boating and fishing. Though camping reservations were required, and the park had only six tent sites, this evening's visitors were in RVs of one sort or another and there was plenty of room for a tent. Austin was only an occasional Boston Red Sox fan yet couldn't drive by the park named in honor of the team's legendary radio voice without stopping for the night. He even had the appropriate ballcap for the occasion.

He continued north next morning and pulled into Billings in early afternoon. He drove and walked around town as usual and eventually settled on what he'd chosen in advance from the Internet as a fitting location: Sunset Memorial Gardens – a cemetery. The grounds had lush groves of trees bordering well-kept open spaces and provided sufficient isolation for an hour of late-night work.

Austin drove to a parking pull-out near the cemetery entrance about ten o'clock. He wouldn't be camping here; officially, it was trespassing, and he didn't want to attract attention. What he was doing now was trespassing, but, he rationalized, not for as long.

He walked to a remote spot on the grounds a far distance from the car where he could work unobserved. He laid out his tarp and began to dig. As before, he dug three feet down, placed the bagged plastic tub flat in the bottom and tested the beacon, then filled the hole leaving little trace of his digging behind. Wind and rain would quickly make it look as it had when he'd begun.

Headlights: a car was driving slowly around looping roads separating cemetery sections.

More headlights: now three cars were slowly driving as if looking for something.

Austin dropped to the ground, collapsed the folding shovel, rolled up the tarp, and put both in his pack. He took a quick GPS reading with his phone, then crawled a substantial distance from where he'd been digging.

Three cars continued their slow progress and eventually stopped about 300 feet away. Figures got out, left cars running with lights on, and walked among the gravestones. Flashlights flicked on, and beams of light stabbed about in the dark as the figures began searching the grounds, steadily working their way toward him.

Austin had the feeling he was in an episode of NCIS or Profiler. He couldn't run or hide so he rolled into a sleeping position and used the lumpy pack as an improvised pillow. Before long, three figures loomed over him, shining lights in his face.

"What'cha doing here, fella?" one asked.

"Just trying to get some sleep," Austin said calmly, holding up his hands to block the light.

"This is a cemetery," said another. "Only the dead sleep here. You don't look dead to me."

"I'm dead tired. Does that count?"

"No, you can't sleep here," said the third. "It may be a quiet place, but it's private property. Is it your car parked back there a way?"

"The Ford?" Austin said. "Yeah, it's mine."

"Then I strongly suggest you get in it and find someplace else for the night. Plenty of motels around with real beds more comfortable than this ground."

"Okay, sorry to be a problem," Austin said as he got to his feet. "Goodnight to you all." He turned, and hearing no objection, walked the long distance to his car and was soon on the road heading out of town.

A close call, he thought. The car gave him away; he should have parked somewhere else. But who would have expected a cemetery Neighborhood Watch this time of night? He drove late into the night, finally stopping for a motel room in Casper, Wyoming.

He continued south through Wyoming next morning. The drive offered miles of emptiness, miles of gently curving roads climbing up and over some slight rise, then gradually descending with the view hardly changing whatever direction he looked.

It was the Nothing.

Austin welcomed the Nothing.

It was a continuing, peaceful view of gently sloping, white-banded uplifts showing many hundred thousand years of sedimentation and erosion; of vast expanses of sparse, brushy rangeland; of huge distant herds of cattle going about their day along with occasional gatherings of horses; of fields of giant white windmills turning slowly if at all; and of fences, everywhere fences.

The Nothing was quiet, silent, like it turned off all the busyness and a tranquil calm settled in.

The Nothing wasn't showy or bossy or noisy or symbolic or clamoring for attention. The Nothing made no judgment, offered no rewards, no possibilities, no alternatives. The Nothing was just there, not requiring anyone's attention or opinion. Whether one noticed the Nothing or didn't notice it made no difference.

Long cloud shadows crept silently across the land.

Wind gusted across the road bending grasses one way then another, but there were few trees to show any movement.

The Nothing was a hollow stillness with just a road leading on to a seldom-changing horizon which neither beckoned nor said stay away. Go there and find another just like it on the other side. Austin could put the car in cruise control and pass through endless empty miles as if traveling noiselessly in space.

He passed thus into Colorado and through seemingly endless downtown Denver, then turned east toward Kansas. Somewhere along the way, in answer to a stray thought he'd had, his mind delivered up a solution for how to deal with two parcels in one trip.

First, drive somewhere at the end of one month, stash the parcel in hand, then send the C. Monica letter and e-mail to have the new parcel sent to General Delivery at the next chosen town.

Second, drive there, retrieve it, put it in its hiding place when the month turned over, then go home or somewhere else that seemed interesting at the time.

The overall route he'd planned had many such opportunities. He could have been doing so already if he'd thought of it, but he'd needed The Road to think in the proper random ways.

The Road had answers.

The Road made the difference.

The Road gave time and space to work things out.

He was digging again at the end of September. He'd driven first through Kansas and Colorado, then Wyoming and Utah, then looped into Idaho and back down to Jackpot, Nevada. There he followed a series of dirt roads south and west to the ghost town of Elk Mountain. The remains of an old mill from a long-ago mining operation still stood there. After roaming the area for a time and seeing no other visitors, he selected a suitable spot atop a large mound and buried Parcel Sixteen.

He sat in his car a long while once he'd finished. It seemed like such a perfect spot. There was no sound, no presence, no disturbance except for an occasional bird call or gust of wind. It was a place completely empty, like no one had been here for 20 years. He'd bury a dozen parcels here were it not for the Rules.

Next, it was on to Boise, Idaho. In the e-mail he later wrote to C. Monica, he asked her to send the next parcel to the motel address where he'd be staying.

With time to kill in Boise, he toured the Bardenay Distillery. Bardenay produced gin, several flavors of vodka and rum, and rye whiskey still aging in the barrels between its three locations. It was also a restaurant and bar serving classic and local craft cocktails – such as a prickly pear margarita – and meals ranging from burgers to tacos to upscale entrees.

"I'll have a Henry McKenna 10-year bourbon, neat," he said to the bartender. "I seldom see something so well-regarded and hard to find at a bar."

"We only have what's left in this bottle," she replied. "Stick around, and you can have another one or two."

"Then you'd better pour me another one now," Austin said. "Also, what's a Bananarchy? I see it here on the cocktail list."

"It's made with banana liqueur, tequila, pineapple juice, jalapeno, a cinnamon stick and served over ice. Shall I make you one?"

"Yes, please do, but after tacos. Could you put an order in for me? I'm starving."

Parcel Six arrived the next day. He loaded it in his backpack, drove to the trailhead he'd selected, and set off equipped for an overnight along the Five Mile Gulch hiking trail. The trail was easy the first mile and a half; then it ground a similar distance upward to the top of a ridge. It was early October now and fall colors were spectacular. Upon arrival, he sat on the ridgetop to view the quiet surroundings.

A hiker came by and stopped to chat as hikers do.

"Lovely time of year to be here," she said. "Leaves are spectacular."

"Indeed, they are," Austin replied. "I'm glad I took time for this hike."

"Not from around here?"

"No, I'm heading east into Kansas."

"Long drive," the hiker said.

"Uh-huh," Austin replied, "but like you said, it's a great time of year, even in Kansas."

"You look familiar."

"So everyone keeps saying."

"You remind me of someone, maybe a long-ago boyfriend."

"I hope he was nice to you."

"He was boring."

"There you go."

She turned abruptly and continued on her way without another word.

I guess I'm still boring, Austin thought.

By dusk, there was no one in sight. He went to a small grouping of rocks a short way off the trail, took a photo of it, then moved them and started digging. The ground was rocky and resisted his efforts. He kept at it patiently and eventually buried Parcel Six using the tarp to leave a clean site as before. He reassembled the rocks to look like the picture and returned to the trail.

It was nearly dark. He could hike out in moonlight or with aid of his headlamp, or he could find a tent spot and go back to the car at first light. He chose to stay. It seemed like an excellent place to lay on the ground and listen to happenings of the night.

Would the night listen to him? he wondered. Does the abyss stare back into you?

Austin didn't believe so. His thoughts began to wander.

Much was written about the beneficial effects of nature, of being in the wilderness, of experiencing the beauty, grandeur, silence, and wonders of the world beyond cities and roads. Thoreau goes on about it, and Muir, Leopold, and countless others soar to rapturous heights to say how much more meaningful life is if one climbs the mountains, hikes the trails, floats the rivers, and seeks out enough blessed solitude to "be here now."

Yes, the advice was sound, Austin thought. And yes, the benefits were real. To be sure, those memories stood apart from everyday humdrum life.

But it was a one-way street.

Nature was indifferent to his presence.

Mountains and rivers and forests went about their business day-to-day whether he was there to see them or not. He could sit on a rock in the wilderness and look at some spectacular scenery and know full well if he'd been there a hundred years before or came back a hundred years from now, the place and the view would be essentially the same.

His presence made no difference.

The natural world went on year after year and century after century offering what many interpreted to be its healing and spiritual properties but it didn't really care, or even notice, who was there to participate.

People frequently say grandly and with great self-importance: "The mountains are calling, and I must go."

No, the mountains aren't calling. Specifically, they're not calling you.

Mountains don't need affirmation; they don't need visitors to be what they are.

People may feel some internal requirement to be among them, but the mountains and forests and rivers don't care if anyone shows up or not.

Night on the Five Mile Gulch Trail began with quiet. Wind rustled gently in the trees and surrounding grasses, but no birds chirped, no animals scolded or called.

They knew something was coming.

The noise Austin made shifting and rolling in his sleeping bag seemed almost intrusive in the near-absolute silence, so he just laid there absorbing the sounds of stillness until he fell asleep.

Rain began around midnight. An insistent light pattering at first, it grew to a steady downpour, then to crashing thumps of fat raindrops on every inch of the tent surface and the ground around it. Thunder boomed like cannons going off; lightning streaked and flared in the sky like giant flashbulbs. Water pouring off the tent rainfly formed puddles, then a flowing stream. Mud splattered the tent walls as huge raindrops splashed continually into the saturated ground and moving water.

Austin lay calmly in his bag unbothered. True, he could have gone back to the car instead of tenting and now been somewhere else, maybe where it wasn't raining. But this middle-of-the-night light and sound spectacle was amazing and he enjoyed being part of it. He slept on and off. The storm continued unchecked, then abruptly ended at the first hint of dawn.

He rechecked the rock pile when he got up to ensure it looked like the photo and found a surprise: cougar tracks in the mud. Sometime after the rain ended, it had walked past Austin's tent, paused there, padded over to sniff at the rockpile, then vanished silently into the brush.

The mountains might not know or care if Austin was there, but the cougar knew. It was willing to share the night's experience without contest or comment.

Austin rolled up his soggy and muddy tent and headed back to the car. Fall colors would be as glorious as they had the previous day, but it wouldn't be the same hike.

Things always looked different traveling the opposite direction.

CHAPTER 9

It May Be One Huge Disappointment

Caroline was talking with David on the phone.

"I took the kids to see dad a few days ago," she said. "Sandra and Rory don't get to see their grandfather much, and they wanted to."

"How'd it go?" David asked.

"Okay, I guess, but I couldn't help wondering where all dad's money is. With this legendary fortune he supposedly has, I didn't see much evidence of it around the house. Art on the walls through the house is nothing fancy or obviously expensive. There are no useless sculptures sitting here and there. The furniture is the same stuff we grew up with and the same with the kitchen. I looked in his liquor cabinet but didn't see anything outrageous there, though I really wouldn't know what I was looking at if there was.

"There's no cook or gardener or driver. It's just dad in his house doing his work, whatever it might be. The place is clean and tidy, but no French maid in net stockings and heels was buzzing around with a feather duster. It made me wonder if he's as rich as we think he is. Maybe it's just an old tale. Maybe he's working every day still hoping desperately for some big break but is more or less broke."

"We're in our 30s, Caroline," David said, "and he still gives us a $5,000 monthly allowance. He would have cut us off long ago if he was struggling. I'm guessing he just doesn't want to show his money off. He never was much for calling attention to himself."

"Maybe so, but for a long time now, I've been counting on the inheritance I hope we'll eventually get to make life suddenly magic and wonderful. Now I'm not so sure. It may be one huge disappointment."

"I've been hoping for a big inheritance someday too," David said, "but there's no point in worrying about it now one way or another. Let dad be dad and live as long as he's able. What happens next is what happens whether we like it or not."

44

"Whether we like it or not," Caroline repeated, sounding somewhat bitter. "I suppose so."

"You took the kids there, you said. So how did they get on with our grand, mysterious, may-or-may-not-be tycoon?"

"They had a good time. Dad broke off whatever he was doing to talk to them. He asked about their interests and activities and school and what they wanted to grow up to be. They chattered away as if they were talking to their friends.

"Everyone got hungry, so I made sandwiches from stuff in his refrigerator and we continued talking through lunch. Overall, the day was enjoyable."

"But..." David said.

"It's been pretty rough going for us," Caroline went on. "Sandra and Rory went back to school last month and it cost a bundle for clothes and supplies. Then, of course, they had to have new computers."

"Computers? They're in early grade school, for goodness' sake. Can they even read yet?"

"Of course," Caroline replied proudly. "When I read to them when they were little, I had an extra copy of each book. They followed along, looking at the words as I read. Then I got simple audiobooks to listen to, and they did the same thing. It gave them a great head start for school. I told dad about it, and he was impressed, or so he said."

"If he was friendly and cordial, you must have gotten there on just the right day."

"I guess so; the visit ended well. But dad never asked if I needed any help. I'd hoped he would."

"Well, sister dear, as dad told me once, more likely several times: we're adults. We should solve our own problems."

"Uh-huh, good luck with that."

With this, they ended the conversation.

David called Juliana.

"Caroline had a revelation," he said when she answered.

"Yeah, I talked to her," Juliana replied. "What she said was maybe interesting but with dad, you never know. He's not much of a show-off. He could be flat broke or have multi-millions and he'd still act the same, just his usual, bushy white, stick-to-business self. Besides, I never cared much about dad's fortune. He can give it to the Home for Homeless Homing Pigeons for all I care. I'm doing fine on my own.

"I went to see him too, by the way," she added.

45

"And?"

"He was pleasant but not very chatty – if anything, even more distracted than usual. I asked if he was okay and he said fine but didn't go into detail. I wanted to review some business decisions I needed to make but he didn't seem in the mood. So, I left before things got awkward. One thing was clear: he is up to something. He didn't say anything but I could just tell."

"And now we can all wonder what it might be," David said.

"Was your car delivered?"

"Uh-huh, but I haven't gone out since then. I thought I'd stay off the streets a while."

"And stay off the weed," Juliana advised. "Jail doesn't suit you, and the room service there sucks."

Their father, subject of these conversations, was in his study pondering a snag he'd encountered. Armored cars had delivered "emergency" cash from his five secret vaults to banks successfully. The IRS got wind of it then and wanted to seize it all, but couldn't produce drug cartel or terrorist affiliations to make a case. The bank's "management of cash procedure" had jurisdiction and was chugging properly along. But even with speedy computers, and even with the stash being split among five different banks, checking individual bills against serial numbers of cash stolen in significant robberies in the last ten years took time.

It was more than a month before their work slowly ground to an end and they notified Xander of the resulting amounts. The service fee was an average of 7.5%, which reduced the final total to a little over $41 million. He provided each bank with instructions on where to wire the money.

And suddenly, after a month of bother and delay, the problem was solved. Regardless of how expensive it had turned out to be, he no longer had great piles of cash sitting around. It was magically now all in Singapore for trusted firms to invest.

A curious thought occurred to Xander Moorhouse.

Who needs an emergency cash reserve of $41 million? What kind of emergency would that be? Some version of the apocalypse? Maybe so.

To think all this time he'd been ready for doomsday and it had never come.

But now, so sorry, the moment had passed. Any impending apocalypse should apply at the next window, please.

He laughed heartily, then went online to his customary liquor store to order a fresh bottle of bourbon.

46

CHAPTER 10

Money Loves Silence

The Republic of Singapore is a sovereign island city-state in maritime Southeast Asia. It lies 85 miles north of the equator off the southern tip of the Malay Peninsula. The country comprises 63 islands and is home to 5.6 million residents who speak four common languages: English, Chinese, Malay, and Tamil.

It is, of course, a tropical country due to its location. Rainfall is abundant, daily temperatures are rarely below 75 degrees, average humidity is 84%, and the sky is often overcast. The best time to visit is winter – November till June – when the weather is clearer and not as hot.

Known as the "Switzerland of Asia," Singapore is a powerful banking hub catering to the economic activity of the whole Asia-Pacific. Its stable political and economic climate, effective legislation and taxation, law enforcement against fraud and money crimes, and stringent secrecy laws have made Singapore Asia's third-biggest Financial Center (after Hong Kong and Japan) and ranked them among the most competitive in the world.

Money loves silence.

Singapore is silent as the grave.

Xander Moorhouse had traveled there six years before. He went unescorted on tours to visit botanical gardens, a cloud forest, a nature reserve, a bird park, Chinatown and Little India, and had seen views of the entire city from a cable car. He'd spent time in a museum of Asian civilization, a zoo, and a gallery of art, and sampled many of the shopping, dining, entertainment, and nightlife opportunities. In three days on his own in a foreign city where people most often spoke English, he got a feeling for the pace and quality of life going on 10,000 miles from home.

He'd then met with investment bankers from seven different high-profile firms. Each glowingly described their offerings and the "modest" requirements of enlisting their services – $250,000 minimum investment – and assured him they would manage his fortune much to his benefit.

None of them sought to influence him with fancy dinner parties, exotic cigars, high-priced liquor, or multiple lovely young ladies. Such things only happened in bad movies, Xander thought, and it pleased him they recognized it wasn't his style. He'd ultimately chosen the three most convincing organizations, gone through the formal process of opening accounts, then traveled back to Oklahoma City ready to carry out his plan.

Now, six years later, his asset liquidation and transfer of resulting funds were nearing a close.

The hockey team had sold at a sensational loss worthy of two days of sports and financial news coverage, and his four office buildings went for huge profits garnering no mention at all.

The 250,000 acres of bare land had gone in a blink to some celebrity with delusional plans of owning most of Oklahoma.

He'd sold stocks, closed most bank accounts, and quickly transferred their balances electronically. Emergency cash reserves – those vaults of paper currency – were also gone.

One downtown apartment building remained to sell along with a warehouse and an electronics assembly plant. Offers were pending; he only had to decide which to accept. Only the movie rights he owned remained, but it didn't matter to the overall plan whether they found a market or not.

Amounts transferred were distributed evenly among the new Singapore accounts and reinvested in international securities not requiring him to own tangible properties. He'd seen excellent results so far. His previous holdings had stagnated at $957 million with a less-than-spectacular growth rate barely keeping up with expenses.

Moving offshore breathed new life into the process. Even without the unsold properties, his portfolio had grown in value past one billion. But he still wasn't interested in telling the world of his success and unwaveringly avoided overtures from the financial press.

Key to the ultimate drama yet to be played out was the young man intrepidly going about the USA secreting parcels here and there. He was six months into it now with ample time remaining. According to reports, he was executing his assignment precisely as directed.

The Seventeen Parcels contained Moorhouse's parting gifts and final words to his children. It was a collection of individual items designed to dramatize life lessons and benefit the three of them in a lasting way. But they would have to work for it.

Sadly, he'd never been much good in the role of a loving dad. Playing catch in the yard, going to their ball games and school plays, comforting them when prom dates were snots or they didn't have one, taking them shopping or to movies, helping them with their school work – he'd "never had time" for such things. He'd been more of a rescue dad buying their way out of problems. The rest of the time he'd "been busy." Their mom drove them to activities, celebrated their victories, and helped, comforted, and reassured them as needed.

They'd grown up first resenting him, then angry at him because their mother had died. Her fatal illness hadn't been his fault, and he was as devastated as they were, but she was gone, they were alone, and they blamed him for it. As they grew up and went their way, instead of filling in for their missing parent, he became more distant from them as he receded into his financial world where success was his reward, failure was his challenge. To them, it was like they'd lost both their mom and dad.

He wouldn't be present to see expressions on their faces when his meticulous Seventeen Parcel strategy ultimately played out. It would happen upon his death when they assembled expectantly in the office of C. Monica Stansbury, Esq. After a methodically premeditated and disappointingly brief reading of a letter he'd crafted, C. Monica would send them off to scour the earth looking for 17 mysterious parcels. Having found them through whatever adventures might be involved and however long it took, they'd return to Ms. Stansbury's office to open them at her direction.

One by one.

In numbered sequence.

Read it and weep or read it and cheer – it would be their choice.

At least, this is what he'd been thinking years ago when he'd devised his intricate plan.

Now he hesitated.

Caroline's unexpected visit had set him wondering. He'd enjoyed seeing her children and spending time with them. But there was something else. Sandra, Rory, and Caroline seemed close in a way he hadn't experienced.

Perhaps relationships with his own children could have been similar. It would have taken only a bit of his time, he now thought. Taken only time to be available to talk or do something together, had he been paying attention.

But he hadn't.

His mind had been somewhere else. Somewhere not including them.

Could these fences be mended? Should they be?

His elaborate parcel scheme had been underway for years and was almost entirely in place. It was far too late to stop it now.

Yet he wondered if it was the best thing to do.

CHAPTER 11

Go Somewhere Else

It was November, and Austin headed south. He wanted warmer destinations through the winter and the first choice was in southeast Texas. He drove I-35 south around Dallas and down through Waco and Austin, then across to Buescher State Park near Smithville. It was late afternoon. He got a campsite and put up his tent.

The park's centerpiece was a 25-acre lake. With limited road access to the shore, he rented a canoe at one end of the lake and paddled slowly to the other end. He turned about then and sought out the wide stream he'd seen feeding into the lake. He made his way up it until he found a flat place to put ashore, then walked a short way into surrounding woods to conduct burial of Parcel Thirteen.

This ritual concluded, he paddled back and returned the canoe, briefly debated whether he should drive downtown for something to eat, then decided he would. He looked for an Oriental buffet restaurant, one where he could choose a plateful of just the things he liked: various preparations of beef, pork, chicken, maybe even shrimp; way light on the broccoli.

Smithville, Texas, population 4,000, probably wasn't the best place to find one. This area was firmly Barbeque and Mexican Restaurant territory. He eventually chose The Blazer Bar and Grill, hardwood floors and ornamental tin ceiling, and ordered a spicy fried chicken sandwich.

The bar looked well stocked. The bartender, who likely also did many other tasks, wore a T-shirt and jeans. Austin ordered a Manhattan with the provision he could specify how he wanted it made: just a dash of sweet vermouth so its strong taste didn't overpower the whiskey, and exactly six drops of bitters. His habitual cocktail snobbery went well beyond crafting martinis, and please don't get him started on bartenders who took dubious short-cuts, like substituting a lime slice for lime juice in a drink or making a Whiskey Sour with lemonade.

As it turned out, the chicken sandwich and Manhattan were excellent.

As he later lay in tenting darkness, it occurred to him he could bring a bottle or flask of something as emergency rations for times when going to town wasn't urgent. But most states had an Open Bottle Law, and he remembered that was why he didn't carry liquor wiᴛʜ him in the first place. Further musing about where to conceal it safely in his car took him peacefully off to sleep.

Next morning, he mailed location details for buried Parcel Thirteen to C. Monica. In the follow-up e-mail, he asked her to send the next one to General Delivery, Pascagoula, Mississippi. The destination was a little over 550 miles straight east.

What to do with a half-million dollars, he thought as he drove.

This was a fresh, new topic, something he'd never had the remotest reason to think about before.

Rule Seven said many things about spending, and he agreed with its logic, but there was surely something quietly outrageous he could indulge in.

He flagged an immediate No to a new car, a house, and a boat. He didn't need or even want those things. No motorcycle, either – no fancy guns, no collections of things in which he'd soon grow disinterested.

But maybe something.

He stopped in Lake Charles, Louisiana, to visit its Mardi Gras Museum, in Lafayette to go on a Cajun swamp tour, in Baton Rouge to tour a French Creole plantation with costumed tour guides, and in Gulfport, Mississippi, to see a model railroad museum. He hadn't the slightest interest in model trains which made as good a reason as any to go there. He finally emerged in Pascagoula after two days of such lollygagging in unbroken sunny weather on the second day of December.

Parcel Two was waiting for him. He stowed it securely in a bus station storage locker, then spent the next two days at seafood restaurants in the general area eating oysters, mussels, chowder, gumbo, crab, jambalaya, shrimp creole, and the whole lineup of delights on various upscale and downscale menus. Finally satisfied, he turned back to the west to drive in no particular hurry to Oklahoma City.

His thoughts still churned about something mildly outrageous to buy or do.

No answer yet.

It would take more time on The Road.

Disaster struck in January.

In Brunswick, Georgia, he woke from a night in a motel room to discover someone had towed his car. The manager didn't know why but told him the tow lot was nearby. Austin elected to walk.

On the way, a mysterious somebody stepped suddenly out of an alleyway, hit him in the head with a bat, and after relieving him of his phone, wallet, and the daypack containing Parcel Four, left him unconscious on the sidewalk.

He awoke in a hospital emergency room. Police had brought him there after a passerby called 911. An officer stood by to take him to the station when his examination was complete. He endured a battery of expensive tests, for which he had no insurance card, and was eventually declared okay.

At the police station, he told what he remembered of the incident several times to several different officers and filled out a report of stolen items. They released him in early afternoon with a copy of the police report, but no phone, no wallet, no money, no credit cards, no driver's license, and even more critical, no Parcel Four.

He went first to a bank. He related his predicament to a teller, got referred to a bank officer who subsequently called in a bank vice-president. Austin was requesting a $500 loan on his Visa card, which, of course, he didn't have. He patiently answered a long stream of personal identification questions, then questions about the incident, then more questions about what purchases he'd last put on the card. He showed them the police report and once they'd read for seemingly the eighth time, finally advanced him the cash.

He next bought a cheap replacement phone, went to a diner with Wi-Fi, and downloaded the application for the locator beacons. After entering the ID and password he saomehow remembered, he brought up an area map. He sent a command to activate any beacons in the vicinity, and two dots came slowly into view.

One would be his car which had beacons in the glove box.

The other could be Parcel Four.

He got a quick lunch then followed the map to the dot's location. The phone started beeping and flashing as he approached, and he soon saw the likely disposal spot: a dumpster behind an auto parts store. Inside it, he saw his pack and wallet tossed on top of other trash. He saw the parcel as well, but it had been removed from the plastic tub, ripped open, and was now empty. The tub and locator beacon also lay loose among the trash.

Austin looked carefully at the scene before disturbing any of it but saw no apparent documents, paperwork, or printouts that might belong in the parcel. If it had contained any cash or valuables, they were undoubtedly long gone.

He retrieved his wallet, pack, and empty parcel and underneath them saw a hardbound book entitled The Moorhouse Family. He recovered the book, then while rechecking dumpster contents for anything not auto parts or office trash related, found two more copies of the same book.

Cash carried in his wallet was gone, but his driver's license and credit cards were still there. He was more or less back in business. He loaded his pack and set off walking to the tow yard.

Austin paid $300 to get his car. He asked why it had been towed but the man on duty didn't know. He briefly considered stopping at the police station with evidence bearing fingerprints they could chase down but chose not to. His case was small potatoes. It was more important to get the damaged parcel back to C. Monica so her client could verify if the books Austin had found were or were not the only thing said parcel had contained. He abandoned the remainder of this trip's mission and abruptly turned about and headed home.

He made an appointment with C. Monica the day after he returned. She met him in the conference room where he placed remains of ill-fated Parcel Four on the table.

"I got mugged," he said in explanation. "Someone knocked me out and stole my wallet, phone, and the parcel. I found it later torn open and thrown in a dumpster. I also found these books there. If they are what was in the parcel, great, but if there was anything else, I didn't find it."

"We're you injured?" she asked, clearly concerned. "Are you okay?"

"Police took me to a hospital, and I checked out fine. I'm good now; even my banging headache is gone."

"Good, I'm glad to hear it. I'll have this boxed up and returned to the client. He can assess the extent of damage and replace the parcel or not as he chooses. Thanks for bringing everything here and explaining what happened. I'm sorry you had such an unfortunate experience."

"Do you have another parcel handy so I can get back to work?" Austin asked.

"I do," and she took one from a stack in a locked closet.

"January is about gone," she said, "you can do this one for February. But as a suggestion, wherever it was you were knocked on the head, go somewhere else, okay?"

They both laughed.

CHAPTER 12

He Hired His Own Investigators

An explosion ripped through the offices and factory operations of EdgeLine Electronics at 2:37 AM February 13. The blast destroyed the entire assembly line, all but vaporized electronic sub-assembly parts worth several million dollars, and destroyed the whole upper floor research lab as the building burned, gradually folded in on itself, and collapsed.

The few workers on duty at the time were on break, some outside having a cigarette a short distance away, some seated in the breakroom apart from the main factory area. Everyone made it to safety with only minor injuries, mainly from the sudden loud noise of the explosion and from falling in their rush to flee the building.

News media covered the story, naming Moorhouse as the building owner. They estimated colossal losses in the explosion and, citing his diminishing property ownership in the USA, breathlessly implied he was near ruin. This disaster could be a crushing blow.

Indeed, it was a disruption, Xander thought. Investigations would drag on, conclusions would eventually go public with great fanfare, and his plan for simple, behind-the-scenes dissolution of assets would not only be needlessly delayed but would attract attention. He wanted to be done with it. He wanted to sit in his study and let the world go by without requiring his participation.

But as he thought more about it he began to see a certain useful side of the situation. He had plenty of time. The Seventeen Parcels Project was nearly half completed and would likely finish as planned. He wasn't off schedule; he was merely being inconvenienced. In fact, it might be well to drag the investigation out even longer.

So, let reporters speculate and postulate and hypothesize and compose nonsensical stories as they were already doing.

The media loved drama.

Demise of the rich was great press.

Let them enjoy the moment, he thought, and wallow in their fanciful depiction of his failure. Their forecast of his impending doom drew attention away from his massive business successes.

EdgeLine took logical disaster-plan steps to recover in the following weeks.

They arranged care and medical checkups for those who'd been injured and submitted corresponding insurance claims.

They rented and equipped office space for a dozen workers, purchased new computers, and restored backups of data stored offsite.

They canceled pending part orders from vendors, canceled scheduled product deliveries, and notified customers the company's line of electronics goods would be temporarily off the market.

They filed a $50 million insurance claim for business and equipment loss, and company executives met to discuss when they could reopen the business, if they could reopen at all.

Police and fire investigators prowled the rubble, along with insurance company agents who appeared on-site seemingly moments after the claim filing. Their work would take months to conclude and produce any relevant results. The lot of them stumbled over each other digging through wreckage and squabbled over jurisdiction and sharing of information.

EdgeLine Electronics also filed a $50 million suit against the building owner, Xander Moorhouse, for inadequate safety provisions and unanswered requests for building repairs. A sheriff's deputy served notice of the suit to Moorhouse about a month after the incident.

Offers Moorhouse had pending for purchase of the building quickly disappeared, and now he faced the expense of leveling the site and disposing of the rubble. Though he thought the bare land could sell for nearly as much, he was still months away from any moves he could make on the matter.

But he knew exactly what to do: he hired his own investigators.

He wouldn't be content with conclusions fed to him by someone he didn't know.

Police and fire finished their work and blamed the accident on building wiring not being up to code and improper use and storage of flammable liquids. They declared the site unsafe and recommended immediate demolition. The insurance company finished up, determining there was no possibility of resuming operations in any remaining building segments. In the end, they made a settlement offer based on cost estimates to rebuild, re-equip, and get back in business.

Months had now passed but the Moorhouse investigators continued their work, consolidating information from other reports with data they'd gathered and mapping out a completely different course to a conclusion.

EdgeLine executives formally accepted the insurance settlement but decided not to rebuild. Instead, they settled outstanding debts, paid severance for employees now out of jobs, then voted themselves a massive bonus from money remaining. Most of them had departed Oklahoma City by the middle of June.

EdgeLine attorneys continued to work the suit against the building owner, displaced employees eventually found work elsewhere, and the company soon passed into non-existence as if it had never been there.

Moorhouse had the building rubble cleared and again put the site up for sale. Offers to buy it resurfaced and the property changed hands within six weeks. He sent proceeds off to Singapore by the end of July.

Investigators he'd hired presented their conclusions six months after the explosion. Finally, after sifting through the mass of detail their reports contained, a clear picture emerged.

EdgeLine Electronics had experienced a significant downturn in sales over the last two years. Their market share had plummeted from 17% to 8%, mainly due to poor quality of their products. Dropping sales had led to purchasing cheaper components, which led to declining product reliability. The company was substantially in debt. A sales forecast showed they would have soon been out of business and would have to file bankruptcy.

Analysis of debris at the site supported conclusions of other investigators on the matter of outdated wiring and flammable liquids but also produced an additional wrinkle: a fragment of a remote detonator. Further analysis established the explosion had been deliberately orchestrated. Company executives, some of them or maybe all, had destroyed their own business to obtain insurance money to cover their massive debt.

Police tracked down and arrested EdgeLine executives for insurance fraud and endangering lives of employees at work the night of the explosion. The insurance company sued to recover settlement money, and the $50 million lawsuit against Xander Moorhouse suddenly went away.

Moorhouse was relieved. As landlord, he'd taken no part in the business known as EdgeLine Electronics. He'd leased them space; they'd provided management, workers, equipment, and assembly components needed to build their products and achieve their business goals.

But they'd failed.

Their attempt to blame Moorhouse had also failed, and their move to loot the company had landed them in jail.

CHAPTER 13

Precisely How He'd Planned It

Austin carried on the Seventeen Parcel Project while the EdgeLine drama played out.

On a late afternoon in February, a month after he'd been mugged in Georgia and a few days after the factory exploded, he drove two hours to Wichita, Kansas, and immediately booked a room at the Marriot Hotel. He then went through an area of parks along the Arkansas River on the west side of town where he located The Old Cowtown Museum, the next parcel resting place he'd chosen via the Internet.

He parked at the Visitor Center and perused displays inside, then paid admission to walk pathways outside. The layout was an old western town founded in 1865, according to a sign. Buildings – including a hotel, general store, saloon, jail, blacksmith shop, Marshal's office, one-room schoolhouse, and nearly three dozen other structures visitors and fans of Western movies would expect to find – were actually built in 1952, but still long enough ago to be suitably bleached and weathered from years of wind, rain, and sun.

Streets were busy. Even in the cool, 50-degree weather, families, some in shorts and T-shirts, roamed from one building to the next, looking through windows and entering to see exhibits.

Austin got a hot dog and sarsaparilla at the saloon, then sat on a bench outside on the main street to watch the three-times-daily gunfight re-enactment between cowboys and ranchers who loudly disagreed about fences and shot each other with blanks.

In his wanderings, Austin noticed trees and brushy forest almost surrounded the property. Board or iron fences closed any openings, and checking further he found strands of barbed wire strung through the trees. No one could get inside the grounds once the Visitor Center closed.

As a result, he selected a spot outside the Visitor Center for his mission. But the museum and grounds were busy; he'd have to come back after dark.

This was precisely how he'd planned it.

He returned to the hotel and sat down for dinner at its Fireside Grille, a friendly, casual restaurant mainly patronized by hotel guests and with an outstanding menu. Austin ordered steamed mussels and lamb chops after minimal deliberation.

To drink, he ordered Macallans 15-year Scotch, neat, which means no ice.

Ice melted and diluted the whiskey.

Master distillers applied lifetimes of experience and decades of continuous effort to produce a product with a signature taste. Who was Austin to disregard this storied heritage? Who was he to think he could improve what they'd created by adding things?

There were those, including nearly every distillery tour guide, who said a few drops of water released hidden flavors and aromas.

He'd tried it.

Several times.

But he still preferred Scotch and other whiskies as distillers created them: straight, no ice, nothing between him and authentic flavor. Let the smoothness or fiery burn or dropping hammer of the taste be itself.

"Even been to Kansas City?" the fellow in a black shirt and maroon blazer near him asked.

"Which one," Austin replied, "Missouri or Kansas?"

"Either one."

"I'm sure I've driven through them."

"There's an excellent restaurant in the Missouri Kansas City called Pierpont's at Union Station, so named because it's actually in Union Station, where you catch trains east or west.

"Pierpont's enormous back bar is nicely designed. The center section is about 12 feet wide and eight or nine shelves high, filled with liquor arranged by type: tequila on one shelf, vodka on another, and so forth. There are maybe 250 bottles there, all lit from behind. There's a library ladder on a rail the bartenders slide back and forth to climb to reach bottles up high.

"Those are just the hard spirits," the man went on. "There are cabinets – classy dark hardwood – to either side holding wine in X-shaped bins, at least 150 bottles and they're nowhere near full."

"Sounds inviting," Austin said.

"Absolutely, and the food is great too. I've been there many times."

Austin checked his phone. "It's a couple of hundred miles from here," he said. "A bit out of my way, but maybe I'll go there on my way home tomorrow. I don't have much else to do."

"You won't regret it, and be sure to order a Singapore Sling."

"A gin drink, right?" Austin said. "Gin, cherry brandy, pineapple juice, and a bunch of other things? A favorite of gonzo journalist Hunter Thompson, as I remember."

"Indeed, such is true. You should check it out."

Austin finished his dinner and, near midnight, buried Parcel Fourteen up and over a bushy mound to one side of the Old Cowtown Museum Visitor Center. The sky rumbled and growled throughout the process and lightning streaked the sky several times, but it was all empty threat. A few cars drove around the parking lot but he was out of sight and was sure nobody saw him.

He enjoyed a luxurious night at the Marriot and, late next morning, headed 200 miles northeast to Kansas City, Missouri. Pierpont's had an extensive and entertaining cocktail menu, according to what he'd found online. It would be a shame to skip such a good recommendation.

Though he'd get there long before they opened, there would be plenty of other things to do in one Kansas City or the other while he waited.

He drove to Riverside, California, in late March. The route took him west across the Texas Panhandle and New Mexico, into Arizona where he veered north to catch a glimpse of the Grand Canyon. He parked at Grand Canyon Village and sat an hour or more at an overlook.

Trails led a few miles relentlessly down to the Colorado River. A person could hike or pay to ride a mule. Walking down, of course, meant hiking back up.

Which was more difficult? Going down used different muscles than going up. Too much of either made you sore.

It was a question for hikers to debate at rest stops or when camped out, along with other trail conundrums like whether it was preferable to hike in rain or snow, whether southern slopes of mountains were easier to hike than northern, or which was better for breakfast: oatmeal or Lump of Wheat?

The Colorado River looked like just another meandering stream from where he sat far above it. But up close it was different, at least according to pictures he'd seen. In a rubber raft, the river took you through rapids ranging from mere riffles to terrifying 35-foot walls of water. There were days and days of it. Some days were calm; others were non-stop, soaking-wet adventure.

He would have to go, Austin thought. The combination of adrenalin rush and peaceful calm while floating through canyons a mile high on either side sounded like an incredible experience.

Maybe – his train of thought now gathered speed – maybe this would be the "mildly outrageous" purchase he'd been looking for.

Was the trip expensive?

Was there a waiting list?

He would find out.

He drove to Riverside, then another 70 miles south to Escondido, California, where he did his usual downtown and outskirts drive-about. A college campus looked intriguing so he parked there and walked around the grounds. He got directions to here and there from students, was invited on an impromptu tour, and afterward continued looking about on his own.

He considered filing Parcel Eight, currently in the daypack he was wearing, behind books on a shelf in the campus library. He quickly ruled the idea out. An ever-meticulous librarian would undoubtedly discover it, puzzle over it a moment, then dutifully mail it to the return-to address. Which meant he'd have to hide it again when C. Monica sent it back as "rework."

He didn't like rework.

Rework was a sign of being sloppy.

When students filed inside the main campus building for a required assembly, Austin declined offers to join them and headed for his car. But he walked past it to the stand-alone clock tower building. With no one visible nearby, he quickly made his way inside the slim, two-story structure and up circular stairs to the clock maintenance chamber.

There he saw boxes of maintenance parts in a tidy stack. One was just the size he needed so he opened it and put its contents in a spare odor-proof bag, sealed Parcel Eight in the emptied box, and put everything neatly back in the stack. He checked the locator beacon on his phone once back at his car, saw a red dot, was quickly back on the road.

He drove the coastal route north through California. He stopped often at ocean and mountain view sightseeing opportunities and in towns for food and local things to do. He had to wait until the month slid into April, so had plenty of time to poke along. C. Monica would send the next parcel to General Delivery in Klamath Falls, Oregon. He already knew where it was going to go.

He retrieved it a couple of days later and continued north. Upon reaching Crater Lake National Park, he entered and drove along East Rim Road from the south. With the massive 286-square-mile lake as a backdrop, he left his car in a parking area and slipped into the woods with Parcel One. It was soon securely in place with no evidence of his work left behind. He resumed his tour around the lake, occasionally stopped to enjoy majestic scenery, then began the 1,900-mile drive back home.

At the end of May, seven weeks later, Austin was in Santa Fe, New Mexico, considering an over-abundance of places to hide the next parcel. There were 96 hiking trails, five bus lines with 256 stops, a dozen or so abandoned and reportedly haunted buildings, 13 cemeteries, 21 campgrounds, a few nearby ghost towns, along with any number of public buildings with wooded grounds where he could easily bury something in the dead of night.

Eleven pawn shops, with names like Happy Hocker, Land of Entrapment, Doc Holliday's Pawn, and Hock it to Me, captured his interest.

But said establishments didn't have much interest in Austin.

One said they couldn't hold a package for more than 90 days. Another wanted Austin to open the package to see what was in it. A third didn't care what the parcel contained but wanted $350 a month in advance to hold it. When Austin said he didn't know how long the hold period might be, the proprietor declined to do business. He finally found a good-natured owner who agreed to hold it indefinitely for $500. He left Parcel Eleven there.

He was in Flagstaff, Arizona, retrieving Parcel Seventeen from General Delivery a few days later, but dealing with it turned out to be even more involved.

He drove from Flagstaff to Wupatki National Monument, an expansive preserve of pueblos former home to an entire civilization of ancient peoples. Instead of one main building usually found in such sites, Wupatki had many ruins among red-rock outcroppings scattered over 55 square miles of rocky desert.

He roamed the site curious about its layout and construction, then set off across the desert to an area about a quarter-mile apart from the main ruins. There he found seclusion in a rocky ravine, and as he'd done before, moved a small rock pile and began to dig.

He dug down to rocks, layers of them. He restored the site as he'd found it and tried somewhere else. It proved the same, so he moved again and again. He eventually found a sidehill spot to dig three feet down and bury Parcel Seventeen. He then carefully groomed each digging site to look as it had before he arrived; he couldn't count on frequent rain to cover his tracks. Finally, he returned to the main tourist area, then to his car, and again to the highway for the two-day drive straight east to Oklahoma City.

He had now successfully placed 13 parcels. The four yet to do would take him to the end of October.

And there it would end.

It was kind of disappointing; he wasn't in a rush for this project to be over.

Then he'd be just a delivery van driver again, not a cross-country, secret mission, modern-day adventurer.

Get over it, he told himself.

Think about enjoying what there was yet to do.

CHAPTER 14

Just Came in to Snoop Around

Austin received the new Parcel Four, a replacement for the one stolen from him six months before in Georgia. It weighed about the same as he recalled, and something thumped heavily about inside when he shook it, so he was content to believe the three books he'd recovered were what it originally contained.

He'd done Internet searching since the incident, searching he probably shouldn't have been doing, but this time with new information to mollify his long-abiding curiosity.

Who was this Moorhouse Family with enough history to write a book about? How did the name Moorhouse relate to what he was doing? Was there some more extensive background to this project he should know?

C. Monica hadn't said much more than "go forth and scatter 17 parcels about the land according to the Rules and get handsomely paid."

Rule One said not to open them but nothing said he couldn't be curious. With lots of drive time each month, questions about what he was doing often popped into his mind, even more so since he discovered the Moorhouse books.

His afternoon research had been fruitful.

A current generation of the Moorhouse family lived in Oklahoma City. Austin had never heard of them, but he was a delivery van driver; why would he unless he remembered taking a package there?

Xander Moorhouse, the local family patriarch, was some kind of genius investor who'd accumulated millions of dollars. Just how many millions nobody knew since he was highly secretive about his life and seldom made the news. He'd lost a ton of money selling a hockey team and just had a building blow up. On the surface, it didn't seem to Austin like stellar tycoon strategy.

Moorhouse had three children, also living in Oklahoma City, who by what little information was public knowledge were thus far dramatically short of being spectacular successes. One owned a business; the others had no Internet news presence except for one who had arrests for driving stoned.

These facts percolated in Austin's mind and gradually led to possibilities.

C. Monica had referred to her client as "he." It sounded a lot like Xander Moorhouse was "the client."

So, what had the two of them sent Austin Somerfeld on a two-year mission to hide?

His actual fortune?

Certainly not.

It would be majorly dumb to put a fortune in any form in boxes and leave them in bus stations and pawn shops and buried in the ground. Pirates buried treasure. How well did that work out? Many of them died before they could come back to get it.

Was he planting bombs?

No, he'd be required to put them in specific sensitive places, not wherever he chose.

But maybe it was something about the fortune. Maybe this grand quest he was setting up was intended to tell some kind of story.

Tell a story to whom?

Most likely the Moorhouse children.

Which implied the day would come when the three siblings he'd read about would set out to find these hidden parcels and try to make sense of them.

Okay, when and if it happened, with a few basic skills they could follow the well-documented trail he was leaving. If they needed help, they could ask.

The sum came to this: he was doing his job, doing what he agreed to do. He was available if needed.

It's how he became famous.

His next destination was 1,300 miles away in Greenville, North Carolina. Late in July, he drove east on highways that were hilly and forested through Arkansas, essentially flat and over significant rivers in Tennessee, and graduating to certifiably mountainous crossing the Appalachians in North Carolina.

It was a stormy day in the Appalachians. Rain beat on the pavement and his windshield and gusts of wind rocked the car side to side. The

66

Appalachians were considered "old, worn-down mountains" he'd learned in grade-school geography, as opposed to the "young, rugged mountains" in the West.

Based on the frequency of steep uphills and downs he experienced, and the numerous mountain passes he crossed over, and the seemingly endless lines of peaks on all sides disappearing and reappearing in angry clouds, and signs cautioning to put on or remove tire chains and be careful on freezing bridges, he judged the Appalachians had still a lot of wearing down to do.

He reached Greenville late afternoon the second day and did his customary drive-around assessment. An abandoned factory caught his eye in the north part of the city. It was a huge brick building sprawling over much of a city block with one-, two-, and three-story levels constructed seemingly at random. Railroad tracks ran behind its length with a siding serving a long loading dock. A similar structure stood on the other side of the tracks. The buildings had a generous assortment of broken and boarded-up windows and a few posted No Trespassing signs. There didn't appear to have been any activity for many years.

He parked his Ford nearby and easily got inside the building. He wandered about the ground-floor space, checked upper levels as well, and in the hour he spent poking around, no one came in to object to or ask about what he was doing.

He found many places to hide a parcel: in cabinets unopened for years since the building had been abandoned, in bottom desk drawers in several office areas, in storerooms and supply rooms with aging contents still on shelves.

But he wanted a hiding place to survive a fire, a potential demolition or renovation, plus possible years of nosey people like himself who just came in to snoop around. Outside on the grounds would be best, he thought, somewhere near the railroad tracks. The tracks would be least affected by whatever events might come to pass.

He got dinner, went to a movie to pass the evening, then returned to the factory in darkness and pouring rain. He located a likely spot across the tracks by headlamp, dug and piled dirt on his well-worn tarp, and completed the soggy burial of Parcel Four inside of an hour.

No trains went by, no police cars prowled the area, no dog-walkers came past to stop and puzzle over what he might be doing.

He finished the task in late-night solitude and retreated soaking wet to his car.

He dried out in a motel overnight and drove north through Virginia in the morning. He crossed the Potomac River into Maryland, poked along through insane stop-and-go traffic around Washington DC, then took the long bridge over, and sometimes under, the Chesapeake Bay to Dover, Delaware. There were 30 or more beaches in the surrounding area and it suddenly occurred to him today was the day to spread out the tarp, eat fried chicken and potato salad, and gaze vacantly out over open water.

The month had clicked over to August. After retrieving Parcel Fifteen from General Delivery he chose a park with a beach, settled down in an uncrowded section, ate the picnic lunch described, and fell asleep.

He was awakened two hours later by a couple in matching dune buggies driving at top speed along water's edge. They raced by and turned, kicked up water and sand with their oversized tires, then sped away. Soon they were back, buzzing back and forth in an apparent effort to cause as much disturbance as possible. They stopped nearby.

"Hi," the man called to him. "How come you're alone out here?"

"It's not a great beach day," the woman added. "We didn't expect to see anyone out at all."

"Just passing through," Austin said. "I stopped for lunch and a nap. I'll be leaving soon."

"Do you live around here?" the man asked.

"No, I drove up from North Carolina just to cross the Chesapeake Bay Bridge."

"It's a scary drive. I never like to do it alone," said the woman.

"It was surely different," Austin said. "I'll do it again on my way back."

"Are you a salesman or somebody with free time for the beach?" the man asked.

"No, a construction worker between jobs. I do carpentry and frame houses."

"There's lots of building going on in Dover if you're looking for work," said the woman.

"Thanks, I'll check it out."

"We should get going," the man said. "We'll try not to disturb you any further."

Then they sped away.

Lying, Austin thought. It was so easy to make up a story and lie to everyone. He was maybe getting too good at it.

He waited to see if they would come back but they didn't. As a precaution, he gathered his things and moved to a spot a few hundred feet away.

Then he dug a hole. Beach-goers often dug holes – to bury each other, look for clams, make sandcastles, or whatever. It wasn't abnormal behavior. He proceeded slowly, placed the parcel at the bottom, then filled the hole just as slowly, methodically smoothing out the sand. He returned to his car after erasing as much evidence of his presence as he could.

He now had a choice of routes for the 1,400-mile journey home: through Ohio, Kentucky, or Tennessee. He sat staring out over the beach to let the sound and smell of the water help him decide.

Then the dune buggy couple returned. They drove to where they'd first seen Austin, stopped, and looked all around. They dismounted their buggies then and walked back and forth. They seemed to be looking for something.

Why would they be looking for something?

They stirred in the sand and inspected everything in a 50-foot radius. Still looking for something, and being obvious about it.

Maybe for something he'd left behind?

They talked to each other a while, then got back in their vehicles, drove back and forth again around the area, and finally went away.

What was that about? Austin wondered. Some sort of Beach Patrol making sure he hadn't left litter?

Would they be back with metal detectors and shovels?

Was there any metal in the parcel?

His elaborate packaging of parcels hadn't included a Faraday Bag to block electronic signals. An oversight on his part, perhaps?

The couple had driven over and left wheel tracks where he'd buried Parcel Fifteen so there wasn't much to be concerned about there.

But Austin wondered.

CHAPTER 15

Alone in the Pitch-Black Dark

A pickup truck shot across the median of I-70 and smashed into Austin's car as he was driving east through Columbus, Ohio, in late September. The pickup driver had passed out from a sudden seizure. His out-of-control vehicle careered across three lanes of traffic, broadsided Austin's car turning it completely around, and left both vehicles wrecked and stalled across the rightmost lane. The pickup driver lay slumped over the wheel. Austin was stunned by the sudden blow and foggily sat trying to get his bearings.

Passing motorists stopped.

Several called 911.

They assisted Austin from his vehicle and to temporary safety at the side of the road. The other driver was unconscious, likely injured, so wasn't moved. Police and a fire ambulance crew arrived within ten minutes, checked the condition of both drivers, and took the pickup driver away to a hospital. Austin was shaken but unhurt, so remained to fill out an accident report as police moved vehicles off the road to allow regular traffic to resume.

Police arranged to have Austin's totaled vehicle towed away. An officer gave him a ride into town and left him at a motel with his suitcase and a large plastic bag containing belongings from the car. Parcel Five survived the ordeal and was in the bag. Austin was now feeling more or less okay but had a problem.

He'd been on his way to New England for a fall vacation trip and to deal with the final two parcels.

Now he needed a new car.

Insurance company, car dealer, something to eat, settle his rattled nerves – he had much to do before moving on.

Relax, he told himself; it could be raining.

He notified his insurance company. A claim adjuster advised him they'd alert an agent in his vicinity and to wait for their call.

He got a burger and a beer, talked with fellow barstool occupants about the crash, then lay down in his room. The new car was a definite puzzle. He had tons of money in the bank, enough to pay cash for a Ferrari or Maserati.

Although such a purchase was briefly tempting, there was the matter of Rule Seven: no ostentatious spending. C. Monica would surely slap him aside the head if he did something so foolish.

A car similar to what he'd been driving would work, but he had to find one, and he was on foot, and his head hurt. He wasn't in any rush; maybe he'd just deal with the whole mess tomorrow.

The local insurance agent solved the problem for him. Scanning the Internet for available used vehicles similar to the totaled Ford, she came up with a suitable replacement and picked him up at his motel in mid-afternoon.

"Sorry to hear about your accident," she said. "I'm Laura, by the way."

"I'm Austin," he replied. "Having my car destroyed wasn't exactly in my trip plan."

"Not to worry, I have just what you need. We're heading to the dealer now."

They arrived to find the dealer had the freshly washed car parked out front.

"Check it out," Laura said. "It's three years newer than the one you had and has all the extras you might need."

"Automatic everything is what I'm used to, and a friendly Map Lady."

"Then this is the one," she handed him the keys, "and it's no cost to you. It's why you pay all those premiums."

"Wow, thank you very much," he said. "You bailed me out."

"Glad to help."

After filling out title and transfer paperwork and getting a welcome night's sleep in his motel, he was back on his way. He drove northeast to Cleveland, along the southern shore of Lake Erie to Buffalo, then across upstate New York to Albany and into Vermont by the following afternoon.

The Georgia-to-Maine Appalachian Trail crossed a highway near Bennington, Vermont, and there it entered the Green Mountain National Forest. Austin parked his new Ford in a nearby trailhead, loaded his pack for an overnight hike, and started walking north toward Glastenbury Mountain.

The trail was serene and quiet compared to the busy highway through New York. Most northbound through-hikers – those walking the entire 2,200-mile path in one season – had likely passed through here by now and southbound hikers on a similar mission were still in Maine or New Hampshire. He was headed for one of the many three-sided shelters along the AT and expected to spend the night alone.

He buried Parcel Five a short distance behind it as soon as he arrived, then took a spot inside. He ate Chinese take-out purchased for the occasion and watched the sky gradually change from blue to pink to orange to dusky black as the sun made its way down.

Soon he was utterly alone in the pitch-black dark lying on a wood-plank shelter floor in the peaceful Vermont woods. But, of course, being Vermont, the sky clouded over and now it was raining.

Silence ruled.

He was warm, dry, safe, and not hungry.

It was the best of times.

Until it wasn't.

He heard faint sounds coming from the trail to the north and saw an occasional flicker of light reflected off wet leaves on trees. A hiker was coming, likely in a desperate press to find shelter from the rain. Sounds grew louder until a bearded, soggy-looking hiker came to a stop at the shelter's front opening.

"It is I, The Great Carmichael, Southbound from Katahdin. I request sanctuary in this holy place of dryness," the young man pronounced.

"Request granted, good sir," Austin said, matching the spirit of the occasion.

The Great Carmichael climbed in, shed his pack and wet clothes, and rolled out his bag in the other end of the shelter.

"I apologize for interrupting your night of blessed solitude," he said, "but it's been a longish day. Twenty-four miles, I believe, or thereabouts. I lost track in the rain and darkness and, of course, the ever-present, soul-devouring, sanity-depleting, oozing, slopping mud. The AT is undeniably the longest river in Vermont."

"This temporary refuge welcomes you," Austin said. "You'll be safe here till morning."

"Are you headed north?"

"I'm not hiking the AT; I'm only here for the night."

"Alas, my intrusion is thus doubly rude. I've dashed your hopes for a night alone. I apologize once more but such is the way of life on a long-distance trail. As compensation, could I humbly interest you in a game of Cribbage?"

"I haven't played in years but yes, it sounds great," Austin replied.

"Huzzah! we play Cribbage and herewith banish torments and demons of the night."

And so it was, candle lanterns lit, game board readied, cards dealt, players warm and dry in their bags, the pitch-black dark of this wet Vermont night became a place of friendly good cheer.

It was again the best of times.

Austin dreamed a Prince of Persia riding an elephant passed slowly by the shelter in the night. The elephant didn't stop. Soon after, Jay Gatsby sped past in his creamy yellow Rolls-Royce with its top down, honking the distinctive three-note horn in passing greeting. A while later, Sherlock Holmes drew up in a horse-drawn hansom cab. He stopped to ask questions about two suspected felons in dune buggies on a beach.

Austin slept on.

The Great Carmichael was up and gone by the time Austin awoke.

… Had he even been there?

… Was his visit just a dream?

What did it matter? Meeting colorful characters on the AT or any long trail was common.

He casually looked for elephant tracks, car tire tracks, hoofprints, and marks of huge iron wheels, but there were only hiker boot prints in the mud, some of them his.

Austin retraced his steps to the road and headed northeast 400 miles to Bar Harbor, Maine. It was now October. To observe the upcoming moment when he'd at last hidden away the final parcel, he planned a few days of lobster, mussels, and chowder (Oh, my) along with driving the sometimes sunny, occasionally misty and foggy roads during fall leaf season and enjoying the smell of food and seawater in coastal fishing villages. By the time Austin worked his way north to Bar Harbor to retrieve Parcel Nine, he was ready for the experience.

Bar Harbor is the gateway to Acadia National Park, a place of picturesque landscapes and low-lying rock-faced mountains. There were summits to seek, trails to travel, and abundant flora and fauna to discover, enjoy, and take pictures of should a visitor so desire. Acadia is one of the smallest US national parks, yet with 3.5 million visitors a year one of the most popular. It is especially crowded during the fall leaf season.

Anemone Cave was once the park's centerpiece but years of tourist activity began to damage its delicate environment. As a result, the attraction is no longer shown on the park visitor map but is findable if one happens to know it's there.

Austin drove along Schooner Head Road, parked, and walked to the overlook where he and a dozen other tourists looked out over Atlantic Ocean water to the Schoodic Peninsula, also part of Acadia Park. He then followed the unmarked path down to the water.

Sea Anemone Cave was just as expected, a cave at water's edge full of many-tentacled anemones waiting patiently day after day through the centuries for the incoming tide to bring them something to eat. He paid his admiring visit and then returned to the overlook to find a suitable parcel hiding place.

But there was still a steady flow of visitors.

He had a long while to wait.

He slept a couple hours, then at dusk entered a brushy area directly across the road from the overlook. He found a secluded and untraveled spot meeting his requirements, alternately dug and remained motionless as a car or two passed by, eventually completed the task and walked back to the car.

And thus, his assignment ended.

He'd distributed seventeen parcels to 17 states according to all agreed-upon procedures and time constraints.

Soon he'd drive home to resume what he'd been doing before his fortuitous appointment with C. Monica Stansbury, Esq.

But that would be days from now.

There was still much to eat, see, and do on the east coast of Maine.

Part Two – Gathering

CHAPTER 16

She Had the Most Beautiful Handwriting

Sydney Bridgewater was a thief.

She was a tall, attractive, brilliant thief with a warm and outgoing personality who dressed impeccably professionally every day, did her job expertly, was reliably there when you needed her, and was always ready to lend a hand at a moment's notice.

But still, a thief.

Stansbury Law Firm had recently hired her as a Computer Systems Analyst to keep computer systems up to date and in top running order. But, beyond those regular duties, she'd soon become everyone's favorite all-purpose researcher. She tracked down cases illustrating obscure points of law, found procedures for doing and undoing complex individual and corporate agreements, implemented methods for filing court cases online and notifying clients electronically instead of generating pounds of printed documents, all of which the individual requesting attorneys could and should have handled, but it was easier to ask Sydney.

It wasn't a problem.

She was glad to help.

In addition to these many positive attributes, and aside from the whole thief business not a single person in the world knew about, Sydney had a distinctive characteristic that immediately captivated everyone with whom she worked: she had the most beautiful handwriting they'd ever seen. Just a routine sticky note from her as reminder of a meeting or appointment was a wonder to behold.

She'd developed this skill because she found the artistry of shaping simple letters fascinating. She did calligraphy artfully and kept a superb assortment of calligraphic inks and pens in her desk at work and home. But this collection paled in comparison to her accumulation of fashionable fountain pens. She had 187 of them, all kept clean and functional, some costing more than $5,000 apiece.

These expensive pens weren't rubber-banded together in a cylinder and tossed in a drawer somewhere. On the contrary, Sydney kept them in flat display cases with individual identifying slots she could stack discreetly in her apartment closet or set out to admire if she chose.

Though her collection had grown large and represented a substantial cumulative investment, it didn't require garages, parking places, licenses, registrations, or regular professional maintenance. It took up little space, had low ongoing cost, and didn't attract attention. It was a satisfying thing to do.

But a collection of 187 luxury fountain pens was just a start.

She always wanted more. Maybe 500, if there even were that many available in the world.

Sydney Bridgewater didn't have a close circle of friends. She saw a colleague for lunch or a movie on occasion, but like herself, acquaintances tended to be people who didn't ask many questions. In conversation, Sydney tended to be blunt and direct and preferred to avoid subjects like relationships, life goals, and what her law firm job had her doing all day.

In truth, when people learned she worked for a law firm, they usually figured what she did was expensively boring.

Also in truth, Sydney would rather go alone to a live roller derby match than talk to anyone.

She came to Stansbury highly recommended. Her previous employers – an auto dealership, a grocery chain, and a heavy equipment auction house, all of whom were identified prominently on her resume (which she termed her "Provenance") – were enthusiastic about what a pleasure she was to work with, about how efficient and productive she was, about her outstanding work for the company, and about how they'd hire Sydney Bridgewater back without hesitation. Each assured the Stansbury Law Firm Human Resources Department that Sydney was brilliant and would be of great value.

What none of them seemed to realize was she'd been stealing from them, all of them, and still was.

At each job, she found ingenious ways through background computer code to redirect a tiny, hardly noticeable fraction of each transaction comprising the company's monthly income on a circuitous, hard-to-follow journey to her bank account. Small, barely traceable amounts each month added up to a few thousand dollars. Said few thousand dollars per month, from each employer, had added up to several million over the years. And it didn't stop when she left a company's employ. Her stealthy program code continued to run month after month even after she'd departed, adding ever more to Sydney's secret stash.

At her Computer Analyst job with Stansbury Law Firm, it only took a few months for the thief side of Sydney to identify an opportunity: the client billing process, the firm's primary source of revenue. The following is a more-or-less simplified view:

- Lawyers report time to a specific case in hours and tenths thereof and include narrative detail of work they've done.
- They also report miscellaneous related expenses: travel time, copies made, cost of documents obtained from the courthouse, and so forth.
- Each month, the computer gathers this data by case, multiplies time reported by the lawyer's rate (ranging from $300 to $1,750 per hour), summarizes individual narratives and amounts by date into an itemized bill for each client, details miscellaneous expenses at the end, and produces a total amount due for the billing period.
- The system then pays amounts due from retainers the firm requires clients to keep on deposit and notes balances remaining therein on the bills.
- Bills are mailed or e-mailed to clients as a done deal: we did this work, it cost this much, you paid this amount from your retainer, here's what you have left.
- Money now "earned" by the firm then passes from retainers to the firm's bank account.

Sydney saw three things she could write background program code to accomplish.

Her program could increase the amount of time reported for each line item by some small amount like .005%. A time of 1.2 hours would thus become 1.206 hours and, at say, $450 per hour, would yield $542.70 instead of $540. With a whole building full of lawyers, each reporting a hundred or more line items per month, such small amounts would add up.

She could open fake businesses with real addresses and phone numbers supposedly providing legal research, court reporting, copy

77

and printing services, and the like, and sprinkle minor bogus charges at random through the billings.

She could implement a small "service charge" or "convenience fee" of $15 for transactions involving client retainer accounts.

Sydney estimated these coding "enhancements" would yield around $15,000 per month. And because of their small individual amounts and low impact on each client, they would likely never be noticed.

Clients like Xander Moorhouse, for example, would neither notice the minor discrepancy nor be concerned if he did. He had $1 million just sitting there in his retainer. There was, of course, the temptation for Sydney to pluck this million-dollar plum, pop it and a few others like it into her bank account, and skip to a non-extradition country like Morocco, Nepal, or Mozambique.

No, she thought without hesitation. It was a rookie mistake and would bring everything crashing down. Instead of being an employed and well-liked clandestine thief, she would be a fugitive running, running, running. Sydney was too much of a pro to be so foolish. A little at a time, slow and steady, was the better and least conspicuous approach.

But she began hearing more about Xander Moorhouse as weeks went on. He was C. Monica's client. Lawyers didn't talk about client business with co-workers, of course, but office scuttlebutt nonetheless provided a framework for speculation.

Moorhouse was wealthy.

He'd engaged C. Monica to conduct some unusual business.

Said business involved a local package delivery driver.

Sydney was curious, but it was risky to ask questions or search client files. She concluded the best source of information was billings sent to Moorhouse over the past two years.

She created a file of these billings and read through them. C. Monica's narratives about work completed were spare and offered only occasional fragments of information to construct a story.

But there was a story, and Sydney gradually pieced it together.

She'd hired an A. Somerfeld in May of the previous year. She'd overnighted something called a "Parcel" to him each month until January of the current year. She'd met with him then regarding an "incident," after which she'd sent a parcel to the client. Regular mailings of parcels to Somerfeld then resumed and continued until September.

Each month she'd received "written communication" from Somerfeld and in October had forwarded "17 unopened Somerfeld letters" to the client. Moorhouse authorized payments totaling $545,000 to Somerfeld throughout the engagement.

Searching the Internet revealed a package delivery driver named Austin Somerfeld. Digging deep into her arsenal of computer hacking skills, Sydney learned from his credit card charges he'd driven each month to various destinations states in the West, South, East, and the far Northeast. She thus inferred he'd been taking these parcels somewhere, then writing letters back to C. Monica to tell her where. But she'd never opened them. These letters were now in possession of the client.

Searches for Moorhouse revealed a variety of conjectures but few facts. He allegedly had a spectacularly successful investment history and had amassed a fortune of perhaps $1 billion. Little had been heard from him in recent years, however. He'd somehow disposed of his wealth as he owned no properties and had no investment accounts in the USA. It might have been moved or invested elsewhere, but there was no confirming information.

In other words, Sydney Bridgewater was too late.

Parcels were gone, and no one but the driver and the client knew where they were.

Was the supposed $1 billion in them?

Most certainly not. It was somewhere, not hidden in mysterious parcels, but somewhere far out of reach.

Dipping cleverly into a billion-dollar stash had sounded promising but was not to be.

At least for now.

She'd keep an eye on Xander Moorhouse. She'd let the parcel drama play out and see what opportunities came next.

CHAPTER 17

He Wanted to Travel

Xander Moorhouse now had nothing much to do. He'd completed his asset conversion and transfer, the Seventeen Parcels were hidden away as specified, he'd prepared instructions for Stansbury Law Firm on handling possible future events, so daily management of his financial affairs no longer required his attention.

This change of life direction was not a sudden surprise. He's seen it coming and had gradually planned for it over the past few years.

He wanted to travel.

He'd gone to Singapore years ago at age 58 and found it a pleasant and instructive experience. There was much more of the world he hadn't visited, so now at 66 and still in good health, he embarked on a series of extended see-the-world trips.

And he invited the children along.

He went to Spain, Portugal, France, England, Ireland, and Scotland with Juliana. They spent two months with tour groups and guides visiting a list of spectacular places they'd only heard of or read about. They ate local specialty foods, drank beer in pubs and whiskey in distilleries, and shopped an ever-present plentitude of gift and trade shops offering local crafts.

At dinner one evening, Juliana asked "Where did you meet mom? Was she your high school sweetheart?"

"I met her in the college library," Xander said. "She sat down across from me and I saw she was carrying a copy of Virginia Woolf's To the Lighthouse. I was struggling my way through The Catcher in the Rye and offered to trade books with her. 'Better yet,' she answered, 'let's both trade them in for something else.'

"One thing led to another from there," Xander said.

"I've tried to read both of those," Juliana replied. "She gave you good advice."

Another day at breakfast, Xander began talking about business.

"I know I've never said so, and I'm sorry I haven't, but I admire your business sense and the accomplishments you've made with your fitness centers. Do you have plans for their future?"

"I won't open any more, I know that. Five separate businesses are enough even though they're all the same. I've occasionally thought of selling them, but I'm not sure what I'd do then."

"That would be a big step; you'd have to think it through carefully."

"Well, I understand you are legendary for bold business moves and investment strategies. You've been an inspiration to me. Maybe you can help."

He went to Mexico, Panama, Peru, Brazil, Chile, and Argentina with Caroline, Sandra, and Rory. The children were thrilled and constantly checked their smartphones to find something new they positively had to see, eat, do, or buy.

"Did you and mom go on trips like this?" Caroline asked as they sat at a café for lunch in Panama City.

"We did but only in the US. We were married when we were 23; you were born when we were 30. I was a newly minted lawyer trying to hold a job and make a living, so trips we took during those seven years were to see things nearby."

"What was it about practicing law that took so much of your time? You were a great dad when we were little, but you kind of drifted away."

Sandra and Rory seemed taken aback their mom would be so blunt.

"I was successful," Xander replied, "and the more cases I won, the more clients I got, and the more money rolled in. The possibilities of this career became intoxicating. I saw a profitable future ahead and got caught up in it. Not to make excuses, but that's the way I was then."

"I guess I can understand that," Caroline said, "but we sure missed you. I'm glad you're doing this with us now."

"We are too," Sandra said. "Seeing such a big part of the world is really fun."

"Will we get down to Cape Horn?" Rory asked. "That's about as far as you can go in that direction."

"We'll go wherever you wish," Xander replied. "I made all this money; let's spend it."

After two months of many different conversations, along with seeing the largest this and the longest that and the southernmost something else and the most colorful birds and butterflies and the most exotic wild animals and a whole associated list of unmatched wonders, everyone agreed they'd had a wonderful time.

David and Becky accompanied him to India, Thailand, Malaysia, Vietnam, and the Philippines for yet another two months. As with Caroline and Juliana, they went to local restaurants and museums and tourist attractions, traveling about the countries on trains, occasional chartered planes, and tour group busses. Becky maneuvered her wheelchair expertly for all modes of transportation and even left it to ride an elephant with a guide's assistance. She declined an opportunity to ride an ostrich in Vietnam, however.

"What did you and your wife enjoy doing together before your children were born?" Becky asked one day on a long train ride.

"We liked going to fancy restaurants to try different things to eat. I remember when we first tried snails and caviar and goose liver. She loved them all, as did I. She was also very fond of bourbon – a big plus in her favor.

"We went to movies a lot. She's the only person I ever met who liked both sappy romances and gruesome horror movies. We also enjoyed sitting in the park eating ice cream cones, especially under an umbrella in pouring rain."

"Sitting here actually talking to you, which must be for the first time in years," David said, "I can't help being impressed. You did something with your life. You didn't let life happen to you. I think I could learn from your example."

"Nothing is stopping you from being good at something," Xander said, "whatever it turns out to be."

Later, and on his own, Xander went on trips to China and Japan, Australia and New Zealand, Norway and Finland, Greenland and Iceland – a month or two each – then on an African safari.

As if all of this wasn't exhausting and satisfying enough for someone whose milestone 65th birthday had already come and gone, he then got behind the wheel of his vintage Lincoln Town Car and drove northeast to Prince Edward Island, then set across the entire width of Canada and north through the Yukon into Alaska.

He went fishing.

He saw glaciers.

He watched totem poles being carved in native villages.

When winter hinted its arrival, he finally headed slowly and somewhat reluctantly south back to Oklahoma City, thus completing the last leg of his 12,000-mile motorcar journey.

He had now seen the world. Though he would likely see different things if he did it again, he'd seen enough in two years of traveling to turn to something else.

CHAPTER 18

Together They'd Build a Business

Said "something else" was a project he'd devised listening to his children during their time with him and thinking through possibilities on his own. When he'd sufficiently worked it out, he called them all to his house to share his ideas.

"Together, the seven of us should build a business," he said to a group looking curious but puzzled, "a business we can create and operate using everyone's contributed ideas. This business would provide each of you a wage-earning job, along with part ownership, profit-sharing, and therefore more certainty for your future."

Seeming even more puzzled now, they were silent quite a long while, glancing one to another as if waiting for someone to respond.

"What kind of business," David finally asked.

'What I have in mind," Xander went on, "is an ice cream shop serving cones and shakes of many sizes, a list of creatively elaborate sundaes, along with hot dogs, burgers, and fries and several varieties of delightfully crunchy potato chips."

"Sounds like an upscale Dairy Queen," said Caroline. "Aren't there already enough ice cream shops and burger stands around town?"

"It's true," Xander replied, "there are other similar businesses, but there's always room for one providing a truly excellent product. Besides, I have an idea to make this one stand apart and become instantly popular: design the building interior to look like a Monopoly board and provide space for customers to play the game."

"Whoa, sounds fun," Becky said with sudden enthusiasm.

"How would it all work?" David asked. "Who's going to do what? I'm sure Juliana knows what to do, but the rest of us don't know the first thing about starting or running a business."

"We'll start together," Xander said. "I'll provide money to obtain a suitable building or building site. Since I am, after all, a lawyer, I'll help you write contracts and obtain required permits and permissions.

"Then your creative thinking goes to work designing a suitable layout for the space. Answer questions like where the kitchen should be, where the sales counter would go, where customers should sit, and so forth. Along the way, you figure out what your actual products will be and how you make them unique. Do those things, and you'll soon have your own business."

"This is a great idea," Juliana said. "I'm certainly willing to participate and I'll contribute what I can, but I already have businesses to take care of."

"I'm in," David said. "Not a doubt in my mind."

"Count me in, too," said Becky.

"I'm not so sure," said Caroline. "Do any of us have the skills to do this?"

"Sure we do, Mom," Sandra said excitedly. "Some things might be hard to learn, but we can do it."

"Absolutely," said Rory. "We're all smart and willing to work."

Rory's and Sandra's enthusiasm carried the day, and everyone agreed to explore Xander's proposal further.

And such is how The Board Room Ice Cream, Burger, Hot Dog, and Potato Chip Parlor got its start. Xander advised such a name from the very outset, one that described what the business itself was. Naming it Duffy's or The Moorhouse wouldn't tell potential customers enough to get them in the door.

Someone had to be in charge. It wouldn't be him, Xander said; this was to be an enterprise for them to run. They talked about it often and finally held a family meeting on the subject. Caroline nominated Juliana.

"You're the only one with business experience," Caroline said, "especially a business with real customers coming in every day."

"I already have plenty going on," Juliana replied.

"We just need someone to get this started and figure out who should do what," David said. "I want to work there, but I need a path to follow; I couldn't be in charge."

"Okay, I'll do it," Juliana said. "I'll need everyone's help so here's what I suggest.

"Caroline, you take care of personnel. Figure out how many workers the shop will need, then use a placement agency to find them.

"David, you handle inventory. Make sure we have enough burgers and hot dogs and ice cream to sell without running out. Start by finding good products and tracking down reliable suppliers.

"Sandra and Rory, at nine and 11 you're not yet old enough to work behind the counter but you can invent a menu and help find equipment to make things on it. The rest of us need to know how to do it too. Caroline, you'll have to find a few cooks with experience.

"Becky, you'll be floor manager. Talk to customers, answer their questions, make sure everything in the shop is running smoothly.

"We'll also need an accountant, someone to keep track of income and expenses and keep us from going broke," Juliana added. "I happen to know a good one, so we're in luck there.

"So," she concluded, "you wanted someone to be in charge. Does anyone have a problem with their assignments?"

"Does it matter if some of us don't know a single thing about what you gave us to do?" David asked.

"Not at all," Juliana replied. "Between now and opening day, you'll have plenty of time to work it out."

They found a suitable building, Xander arranged its purchase, and what they were now simply calling The Board Room proceeded gradually into existence over the following year. It featured a game board painted in detail on the floor (Becky's idea), connecting to booths around the perimeter identified with property group colors and themes (Caroline's idea), sundaes named Go to Jail, Chance, Free Parking, and the like (Rory's idea), Monopoly money coupons given with food purchases good for buying game houses and hotels (Sandra's idea), and (this was David's idea) a room in the back with tables for Monopoly games and tournaments.

A momentary snag had been Parker Brothers, owner of copyrights to the game. Though the mechanics of playing the game weren't under copyright, the Monopoly name and board artwork were. They thought this to be a setback at first, but David solved the matter instantly.

"I happen to have an official Monopoly variation based on Oklahoma City," he said. "It has the same board layout and rules but with Oklahoma City locations and buildings as its properties."

Xander quickly negotiated permission to use it as their theme. "Go" was now Land Run, "Jail" was now Traffic Jam, "Railroads" were prominent city streets, but the game played the same.

In place of the copyrighted white-mustached Monopoly Man's figure with a cane, black jacket, and top hat, they used a caricature drawing of bushy-white Xander Moorhouse himself, complete with black-framed glasses, white shirt and colorful tie, and a stereotypical fat cigar.

"I have a special request," Becky wrote to Xander in an e-mail. "I'd like a motorized wheelchair designed to look like a shoe, one of the original Monopoly game pieces. It will surely attract attention. People will want to talk to me, especially if I wear a black top hat. The novelty of it will help sales."

The senior Moorhouse loved the idea and immediately set to find someone to build it.

The Board Room Ice Cream, Burger, Hot Dog, and Potato Chip Parlor opened with a barrage of publicity and became instantly popular. Customers mobbed their opening day and came back regularly after that. Some were there for a hot dog, some to play Monopoly, some just for potato chips. Of course, everyone came for ice cream.

People loved Becky's Shoe-Mobile, especially when she drove it around the Monopoly board painted on the floor. She wore the black top hat, of course, with a black blazer, and every news article and publicity piece featured her picture.

She'd also added a much-needed service. Whenever a customer experienced freeze-up from eating ice cream, they'd press the Brain Freeze button at their table. An alarm would sound, Becky would replace her top hat with a nurse's cap and come rolling up in her wheelchair to offer hot coffee, tea, or lemonade. Another wait-staff member would offer to wrap the person's head with hot towels. The hot drink would end the brain freeze; the rest was drama, turning an unpleasant experience into something fun.

Whatever the reason people came to The Board Room, they brought a hefty cash infusion for everyone who worked there.

The family had jobs that brought them paychecks.

They had something fun and exciting to do.

The business grew and prospered and its popularity seemed destined to continue. Family members worked every day along with others hired to help keep pace with a steady flow of customers. Everyone got their fill of hot dogs and other items from a menu that never changed except for occasional new flavors of ice cream and chips.

But after three years it had become too busy and needed to expand. Now 14 and 12, Rory and Sandra worked there after school and on weekends to help keep up with the booming business, but the place simply needed more space for customers and players.

And not just another basic room with card tables and Monopoly boards.

It required a plush, formal space for tournaments and rental to upscale, big-tipping players who wanted to bring a large group, play an intense day or evening of Monopoly, and be waited on with constant refills of food.

The partners – Juliana, Caroline, and David – purchased the building next door. It had a similar structure which allowed them to turn the two buildings into one, remove center walls, and extend the sales floor to occupy the entire expanded space.

They had the Oklahoma City Monopoly Board layout repainted on the perimeter of the enlarged floor. Since game properties were specific Oklahoma City locations or buildings, they had hazy silhouettes of each painted on the wall connected to its property.

The expanded space contained more than twice as many booths and tables as before, all grouped in the center of the vast rectangular room. The single sales counter became two – one for food, one for ice cream – and they added two more rooms with tables for players. As a result, Becky Moorhouse now had twice as much space to zip about in her black top hat, blazer, and Shoe-Mobile as she oversaw the operation.

The most significant change came in the unused basements. Both were entirely gutted, dug eight feet deeper, and joined into a single, massive, high-ceilinged room. Elegant wall-coverings, vintage lighting, and comfortable leather furniture converted it into the fashionable tournament and high-roller game space they'd imagined. In addition, they had both an elevator and a dumbwaiter installed so wait staff wouldn't have to go continually up and down stairs.

Construction took nearly a year to complete. The Board Room remained open every day and staff worked around inconveniences with business-almost-as-usual good cheer. As soon as the expanded space officially opened, new cash began pouring in. The Bunker, as they named the new basement room, soon became one of the top hotspots in town.

The senior Moorhouse had only an advisory role in managing day-to-day business, and took no payment from it, but was involved with the family every day. He was pleased with their tales of daily blunders and triumphs and was complimentary about their hugely positive cash flow. He offered advice when asked but otherwise allowed them to work through their problems and learn from their mistakes.

He insisted on only one unwavering business practice: Pay your bills. Good credit and good relations with suppliers were vital to success.

This daily involvement gave him many hours to reflect on how his life was now different. Relationships with his children had dramatically changed since the day Caroline came to visit with Sandra and Rory, since the months he'd spent traveling with them to remote places on the globe, and since they'd all taken up aprons and scoops to sell ice cream. It had been a pleasing transformation that brought him a small measure of contentment at long last. After being inattentive to them during so much of his life, he thought perhaps he'd managed to improve his behavior in some perceptible way.

But there were side effects.

This "transformation" now made particular contents of the long-hidden Seventeen Parcels obsolete. What he'd at first thought to be a fitting way for his strategy to play out now seemed unduly harsh. The "read-it-and-weep" plan he'd devised for bequeathing his fortune needed to be revised.

He thus rewrote his will over two thought-filled days. Once completed, he carried the finished copy personally to the Stansbury Law Office, had it notarized as authentic, and in the presence of C. Monica, Esq. assembled a new Parcel Seventeen.

"This replaces the one I first gave you," Xander told her. "Please seek out the original wherever it may be and replace it. Of course, the usual rates of compensation apply."

"I'll take care of it at once," she said, and after Moorhouse departed, contacted Austin.

"I have additional parcel work for you," she told him on the phone.

"Great," he said.

"First, one question: do you know who my client for this is?"

"I've made some guesses," Austin replied.

"Have you ever tried to make contact?"

"No, my business is with you."

"Good, I'd appreciate it very much if you kept it so."

"The additional work I mentioned is this: there is a new Parcel Seventeen. You hid the original somewhere nearly six years ago, according to my records. I want you to go wherever that somewhere is, retrieve the first Parcel Seventeen and replace it with the new one I have here. This assignment comes with the usual $25,000 payment, by the way."

"Finding the first one shouldn't be a problem," Austin said. "I'll pick up the new one from you today."

He checked his notes from six years before: he'd buried the original in ruins at Wupatki National Monument. He prepared for traveling, picked up the parcel, and headed to Flagstaff, Arizona. It was a 13-hour drive straight west.

The parcel's locator beacon drew him unerringly to the site when he arrived there the following day. He dug up what he'd buried and removed the original Parcel Seventeen from its packaging. After repackaged the replacement, he buried it and refilled the hole. Assignment complete.

He notified C. Monica by e-mail and advised he'd return the replaced parcel to her.

She was pleased.

A final wrinkle had been ironed out.

CHAPTER 19

Find What It Is, and Where It Is

Xander Moorhouse died four years later.

He took suddenly ill and his heart function steadily deteriorated over just a few days. He called 911 when pain and difficult breathing didn't subside and medics quickly took him to the hospital. The head nurse called Caroline, his emergency contact, and the concerned family gathered day by day at his bedside. Xander Moorhouse passed on soon after.

Juliana arranged a memorial service and requested family members to attend. It was four days away.

"Mom," said Sandra, "you need to go shopping."

"I suppose you're right," Caroline replied.

"We have this memorial service for grandpa to attend, and then you'll likely go to the lawyer's office to read whatever he's left for you. You can't go either place in holey jeans, sneakers, and a sweatshirt. You need something more appropriate."

Sandra had grown up partly in the shadow of her brother, yet had developed a definite, distinct, and very pleasing personality.

She did well in school and was popular with her classmates. She liked to build things and solve things and discover things. She was excellent at running and target shooting and had a modest collection of awards from school and local competitions.

She occasionally picked on her brother, mainly for the fun of it, mostly to get a reaction, but she knew when to let it go. The two worked well together and gave each other support and encouragement. She appreciated Rory for being protective of her.

Sandra was tall, thin, athletic, and very attractive. She was a curly-haired blonde like her mother, but unlike her mother, she liked to dress up and look nice. Pretty clothes made her feel like somebody instead of an unremarkable nobody. As a result, looking sharp every day at school meant no shortage of interested boyfriends.

"What should I get," Caroline asked. "I never pay much attention to what I'm wearing."

"Ya think?" replied Sandra. "Let's go together and I'll help you."

Sandra steered her mother confidently from store to store and they made many purchases, sometimes over Caroline's objections.

"I doubt I even *own* a dress but why do I need three? Isn't one enough?

"Two pairs of heels? Stilettos yet. I don't think I can even *walk* in them!"

"Stockings? Who wears those anymore?"

Sandra reassured her in each case what she'd chosen for the new dress-up version of her mom – "You can't wear the same dress everywhere." "Stilettos have four-inch heels and higher; these are only three." "Bare legs are fine with strappy sandals but not with a formal outfit." – was the right way to go.

"Your brother and sister won't even recognize you," Sandra said. "Wouldn't *that* be totally worth it?"

The entire contingent of family members gathered at the memorial looking appropriately solemn, along with family friends and several of their father's business acquaintances. A few spoke at the service but only in generalities. Xander was secretive and no one knew much about him. To fill the seeming void, Juliana stepped to the front of the group.

"Xander Moorhouse was our father," she began. "He became distant from us when he was practicing law and more so after our mother died. We resented him then, but for the past ten years he's been the kind of father everyone would want. He traveled the world and took us along.

He helped us start a business. He let us run things the way we wanted and didn't get in our way. He helped us learn from our mistakes.

"We've been successful, largely because he steered us in the direction of success. Success was a place he recognized, a place he felt comfortable. He knew how to get there. We were privileged to have him as our guide. We'll remember dad that way, as our guide, and we'll miss him helping us."

They buried him next to their mother in the family cemetery plot that afternoon. There was a brief newspaper obituary, which Juliana wrote, but no mention of him in financial news. Moorhouse had exited the local and national economic scene years before. It was as if he no longer existed, which, of course, now he didn't.

And – bonus points to Sandra for this – neither David nor Juliana recognized Caroline at first.

92

"You look fantastic," Juliana said to her.

"You certainly do," David added. "Great outfit."

"Thank you," Caroline replied, still a little wobbly in her unaccustomed heels.

Such compliments were a new experience.

They made her feel sort of good about herself.

Days later, C. Monica notified the three siblings to gather in her office on a Tuesday afternoon. They found workers to cover their duties at The Board Room and arrived promptly for their appointment.

"Welcome," the attorney said in a somber tone once they were seated in the conference room, "please accept my sincere condolences upon the loss of someone so close." The three Moorhouse heirs expressed their thanks.

"We're here to carry out the final wishes of your father, Mr. Xander Moorhouse. What I have here isn't his actual will; it's a letter he gave me some years ago for this meeting. I'll read it to you."

> To my children Caroline, David, and Juliana:
>
> I have known and accepted that I was not the kind of father you thought you wanted for most of your lives. I make no feeble effort to apologize; it was my choice at the time. Life was all business to me then and so it will be here today.
>
> I bequeath to you the following:
>
> First, the family home: I leave it and its contents to the three of you to occupy or dispose of as you agree among yourselves.
>
> Second, my accumulated fortune. I leave it to you in its entirety. However, first you must find *what* it is and *where* it is.
>
> My attorney will direct you in this effort and explain accompanying terms and conditions.
>
> Farewell to you, my dear children.
>
> (Signed) Xander Moorhouse.

"The end?" said David, astonished. "He said nothing else?"

"It's all the letter says," C. Monica replied. She handed them each a copy.

"We have to *find* it?" said Caroline, clearly upset. "How are we supposed to *find* it? Find what, exactly? Looking for something certainly isn't what I was expecting."

"This is weird," David added. "We don't even know what to look for."

"I think Ms. Stansbury is about to tell us," Juliana observed.

"Yes, I am. Please listen carefully, all of you. What follows is what your father instructed me to tell you."

The three heirs fell silent and devoted C. Monica their full attention.

"Information about your father's fortune," the attorney began, "and guidelines for its use and disposal can be found in 17 parcels secreted in various places about the USA, each in a different state. I have letters concerning the whereabouts of each parcel sent here by the individual who hid them just over ten years ago." She handed David a large brown envelope.

"None of the letters are opened. They contain detailed information about where to find each parcel plus any items needed for its retrieval. You may open the letters and use them in your search. The envelope they are in also contains an expense check for each of you for this effort."

"Our *search*," said Caroline. "We have to go *looking* in 17 states to find these things?"

"Yes."

"Can we hire someone to do it, like maybe the person who put them wherever they are?" asked Juliana.

"A person named Austin Somerfeld who lives here in town, or at least did ten years ago," David said, reading from envelopes in the brown packet.

"You may contact Mr. Somerfeld as you wish," C. Monica replied, "but your father was emphatic in this matter about three things:

"First, you must cooperate and work together to find these parcels.

"Second, you must not open any of them until you've gathered all 17.

"Third, you must not tell anyone what you are doing. The last thing any of you need is an army of reporters with cameras and news vans following you around the country.

"Actual opening of the parcels will take place here in this office, proceeding in parcel number sequence, once you've located them all and brought them home."

"As I said," David observed, "this is way weird. Do you happen to know how much this supposed fortune is worth?"

"I have no idea whatever," C. Monica said. "This office did not manage his finances. It might be zero; it might be billions. It might be under a mattress; it might be at the North Pole. These details are what your father tasks you to find."

"So," David said, "to be clear, this envelope of letters directs us to 17 hidden parcels which, when we find them, and eventually open them, somehow tell us what his fortune is and also where it is. Which is what dad's letter said we had to do, correct?"

"Correct, to the best of my knowledge," C. Monica said. "I don't know what any of these parcels contain but I do have two things to give you to use.

"First, here are a dozen of my business cards to distribute among you. If you get into some problem situation and need assistance, call me. I'll help you out any time of day or night.

"Second, on the table by the door are prepaid mailing boxes. Each time you locate a parcel mail it directly to me as soon as possible. Doing so will avoid any potential loss due to theft from your car.

"Regarding ongoing communication throughout this effort, one of you please notify me regularly of your progress. I'm very interested. I'd like to know how you're doing.

"In conclusion: I have now delivered everything I was instructed to give you and relayed all information I have. It's up to the three of you now."

Caroline, David, and Juliana looked at each other silently a long moment, then got up and departed.

"Let's get a drink," David said. "I think we could all use one."

CHAPTER 20

It's Just Dad Being Dad

"So much for being suddenly, fabulously, mind-bogglingly rich," David said. "Now we go goose-chasing around the country on some scavenger hunt." They were sitting at a bar drinking martinis, straight whiskey, whatever came to mind.

"As I already said, it's not what we were expecting, that's for sure," said Caroline, still visibly upset. "And to think I got all dressed up for this!"

"These letters are all from the same person, just like the attorney said," Juliana noted as she dug through the brown envelope, "and there are indeed 17 of them, and they're all numbered. It's all neat and tidy. What do you suppose we should do first?"

"I don't want anything to do with them just now," Caroline said. She sat silently fuming for a time, then added: "but I suppose I could give them to my kids. They're both good at puzzles. Maybe they can make some sort of map of where to go or something, although it's hard to imagine any of us going anywhere."

"Sandra and Rory would be perfect for this," David said with some relief. "Yeah, get them busy on it. I don't think I'm ready for any detail work right away, either."

"Rory is what, 18 now?" Juliana asked.

"Yes," Caroline replied, "and Sandra turned 16 several months ago. They both live at home, do well in school, and work at The Board Room whenever they have spare time. I do have to say this ice cream shop, however strange the idea might have sounded at first, has taken off and made a big difference in our household budget."

"Very true," David said. "I wouldn't have believed it, but sometimes I feel just the slightest bit competent working there and talking with the customers.

"Anyway, back to your kids, the map idea might grab their interest.

Real-life buried treasure and all. Go bravely forth and dig up riches. They could give us a start on this undertaking, whatever it's supposed to be."

"Do you have a problem with this, David," Juliana asked, "like it's a big joke or waste of time or something?"

"No, it's just dad being dad again. He couldn't straightforwardly do anything but had to create all this drama. Why couldn't he just tell us what's going on? Why did he have to turn it into some bizarre mystery? About all we've gotten from his allegedly fabled riches so far is: don't quit your day job."

"Dad wrote the letter we heard today ten years ago, maybe even before," Caroline said. "How is it even relevant today?"

"Maybe it's just what he was thinking back then," Juliana said. "A lot has changed since."

"Whatever," David said, "maybe Sandra and Rory can help make it more understandable."

They each ordered another drink.

Rory Michael Griffith was a high-school senior and captain of the wrestling team. Though he was short and beefy and often looked like a street thug, he was gracious and showed much intelligence in class.

He liked to read. He enjoyed solving mathematical puzzles. Word problems were fun, he thought – they were a matter of parsing out which pieces of information were helpful and which were not, then forging on to the answer. He was cheerful and had an optimistic attitude. He knew whatever happened he could make things work.

Rory didn't care about fast cars or motorcycles or playing in a band, and as a child, had no interest in dinosaurs or being a fireman. But he did enjoy welding. The family's backyard had several curious sculptures he'd been creating from large and small scraps of metal.

He'd gotten into the usual amount of teenage trouble. He'd once shoplifted cigarettes and another time a pint of whiskey. Youthful lessons learned on these occasions were: cigarettes tasted awful and made him sick, whiskey was apparently an acquired taste but why would anyone want to, and shoplifting took skills he quickly decided he'd be better off not learning.

He was popular with kids his age and had many close friends, including more than a few girls. He protected his little sister when she needed it, making it clear picking on her would bring the same consequences as picking on him.

Both he and Sandra realized at once what was at stake with their grandfather's will and got to work. They opened the 17 letters and read them carefully, tagged enclosed claim tickets and keys with parcel numbers, and searched the Internet for the city locations given.

They began work on a map and by the next afternoon had produced one showing the 17 locations involved, each annotated with the parcel number, its GPS reading, and directions to the parcel's specific site.

They arranged map points in two huge loops showing optimum driving sequence, one going west from Oklahoma to California, then turning north to loop through Oregon, Idaho, Nebraska and back, and another heading east to Texas and Mississippi, then up through North Carolina, Maryland, Vermont, and on to Maine and back.

"This is an elegant piece of work," Caroline said as she examined it. "It's very nicely done and I'm sure it will be helpful." She paused a moment. "Y'know," she went on thoughtfully, "this is starting to sound the tiniest bit interesting. I haven't been to any of these places."

"Mom," Rory said, "seriously, we'd like to go along."

"It's a super road trip, Mom," said Sandra. "We could help find grandpa's fortune."

"Since you brought it up," Caroline replied, thinking about the possibilities, "having you along sounds like an excellent idea. Dad said we should all pitch in to do this, which includes you two as well."

She called David. "We have a map to look at," she said. "Should we all meet up to look it over?"

"Definitely," he answered, "and I'm thinking we should get hold of this Somerfeld guy and see what he can tell us."

"Okay, how about tomorrow night at my house? Everybody bring a pizza."

Nearly ten years had passed since Austin's mostly enjoyable two summers of secreting packages around the USA. He'd driven over 25,000 miles on that project and ended up with a pile of money, a newer car, and many experiences to remember. He'd traveled through a lot of country he hadn't seen before.

He'd since gone on the Colorado River float trip, the quietly outrageous "go somewhere else" trip he'd wanted. For ten days, he'd floated enjoyably through a mile-deep canyon with not a single place to spend any money.

He'd traveled to Alaska, Hawaii, Switzerland, and Bermuda, booking pricey tours and staying in $250-a-night hotels. But even though he'd gone to expensive restaurants and ordered snobby high-priced drinks, he'd kept to himself and paid by credit card.

The sum of these indulgences had little impact on his cash reserve. He was still operating under the radar, still invisible, hardly noticed by anyone. Living in such a fashion had become his preferred way of life.

Austin had worked at many driving jobs since then, including operating massive earth-moving equipment (bulldozers, scrapers, excavators, and huge dump trucks), driving a bakery truck on early morning deliveries (it always smelled so good), and chauffeuring local celebrities and business executives around (many genuinely nice people mixed with a few self-important, bozo elitists). He didn't need to work, but he enjoyed it and it felt odd not to be doing something productive.

He still lived in Oklahoma City and was again driving a package delivery van several days a week. His cell phone rang.

"Hi, Mom," he answered, recognizing the number. "I'm out delivering, so I can't talk long."

"Some fellow named Moosehouse or Morhaven or something is wanting to talk to you. He called me just now. You want to call him back?" Austin had seen the obituary in the news so knew who she was talking about.

"Yeah, Mom, text me the number, will you?"

"Sure, I think I can. How are you doing? Everything going fine with you?"

"Great, but I have a whole load of packages here to deliver, and I'm running a bit behind. I'll call you later, okay?"

His mother said okay and hung up. Moments later, a text message came with the number. Austin delivered a dozen more packages, then paused before continuing and returned the call. He talked briefly with David Moorhouse, accepted his invitation to dinner the following evening, and said he'd bring beer.

He'd always known the day would come when someone would want to find what he'd hidden.

This was it.

He could be helpful to them, so maybe they'd hire him. Or perhaps they'd figure they were smart enough to do it on their own. Maybe they were.

The following evening, he pulled up to the address David gave him, figuring he'd offer his help and see what opportunities arose.

CHAPTER 21

We All Have to Find Them Together

A pretty young girl with blonde hair and a hint of red lipstick answered the door.

"I'm Sandra," she said with a friendly smile, "you must be Austin."

"I am."

The group welcomed him in, made introductions, and settled down at the kitchen table for pizza. The beer Austin brought quickly passed to everyone, including the teenagers. Questions began at once.

"So," said Juliana, "you drove these mysterious parcels around hiding them?"

"I did."

"How long did it take?"

"I had two years to finish but got it done in eighteen months."

"Why so long?" Caroline asked.

"Rules," Austin said. "I could only do one a month."

"Did dad tell you that?" asked David.

"I never met your father. I worked at the direction of his attorney."

"Yes, C. Monica Stansbury, Esq., with her huge law firm," Caroline said, "we've met her. Knowing dad's extravagant way of doing things, I presume he paid you well to do this."

"He did." No one asked how much, and he didn't volunteer the information.

"Did you ever see what was in these things?" David asked.

"No," Austin replied, "parcels came to me sealed with a number written out on them in red letters but otherwise no identification. The attorney said she didn't know what was in them either. I was instructed never to open them, and I didn't." He chose not to go into the misadventures of Parcel Four or the replacement of Parcel Seventeen.

"How do we know they're still where you put them?" David asked.

"You don't," Austin replied, "but chances are good they're still there."

100

"Well," began Juliana, "it appears dad wants us to go find them. We'd prefer to send you after them for us, but we can't; we all have to find them together."

"But there's no reason we can't have you help us," said Caroline.

"What would you like me to do?"

"Start with this," and she handed Austin the map Sandra and Rory had prepared. "My kids made this with information from letters you sent to C. Monica." Austin looked it over for a time.

"Excellent work here," he said in a complimentary tone, "but a few things have changed since then. Parcel Eight, for example, the one I put in the clock tower. The tower blew down in a windstorm five years ago. The person who maintained the clock searched for its parts in the rubble and found the parcel. He mailed it to C. Monica using the return address I put on it, she sent it to me, and I took it back and buried it nearby in the Elfin Forest Preserve.

"The bus station in Pascagoula had a general locker cleanout three years ago and Parcel Two went back to the attorney. So, I rented a lockbox in a casino in Biloxi and put it there.

"Let's see, yeah, Parcel Twelve. The pawnshop in Muskogee I left it with changed owners. The new proprietor sent it back along with a bill for $3,500, which I presume C. Monica paid. I took it back and buried it on the grounds of the Muskogee War Memorial. Everything else should still be in place."

"Okay," David said, "so there's one left at a bus station, another at a pawn shop, another at a casino – those we can get on our own. But the rest, are they hidden in some remote spot or buried in the ground somewhere? How do we find them? How do we know where to dig, or if an animal hasn't already dug them up?"

"Good questions," Austin answered. "Here's information I'm sure will help.

"First of all, the parcel itself is a black plastic box the size of a ream of copy paper, and they're all the same. Each is in a heavy plastic bag specifically designed to block odors, then it's sealed in another plastic tub and that's put in another odor-proof bag. The packaging makes the result a third again larger.

"They're buried three feet down. A dog on a leash wouldn't have time to dig so deep and whoever was walking it wouldn't let it do so. Some larger animal might, but with the parcel's Coat of Many Colors – what I called its packaging – it's unlikely any animal will even catch a whiff of it.

"As far as where to dig, each tub has a locator beacon in it. Download the software to your phone and it will show where a parcel is on a map once you get within a half-mile of it. Go to the spot and dig."

"It *sounds* simple enough," said Juliana, "and I have to say you were certainly very thorough."

"I figured someone would want to find them someday," Austin replied, "so I tried to make locating them relatively easy with the right tools.

"I'll give you one piece of advice, if you don't mind," he went on: "it's the middle of May. You should at least get the northern cities done while it's warm. But if you want to do this quickly, you can gather all the parcels in a week or two if you plan it right."

"Here's a suggestion," Caroline said. "We have three cars. If we divide this up, we can work more efficiently and get it done soon."

"Great idea," said Juliana. Then, to Rory, she said: "Both you and Sandra have drivers' licenses, don't you?"

"Yes, we do," he replied eagerly.

"Just got mine a few weeks ago," Sandra said.

"So, if Rory goes with David, and Sandra goes with Caroline, you'll have relief drivers and two heads to work through what to do at each site."

"What about you?" Caroline asked.

"Well, this might be a bit awkward," Juliana replied, "but maybe Austin and I could team up. Does anyone have any thoughts on the subject?"

"If he has time and doesn't charge too much," said David.

"I won't charge anything," Austin said. "I'm glad to help out and see this puzzle to its end."

"What about Becky," Rory asked. "Is she coming along?"

"She's become the face of The Board Room so is there nearly every day," David replied. "I'm sure she'll want to stay behind and keep the place running like she always does. But to keep her involved, I suggest we call her every day from the road with our progress. She can then report to the attorney."

"We have a plan," said Caroline. "As much as I never thought I'd say this, let's go get it done."

"Looking at the map you made," Austin said, "here's how I think we should proceed.

"Caroline and Sandra take the south route and stop in Nebraska, Kansas, New Mexico, Arizona, and California.

"David and Rory head east and do Mississippi, North Carolina, Delaware, Vermont, and up to Maine.

"I'll go with Juliana for the north country: South Dakota, Montana, Idaho, Nevada, and Oregon.

"It will be five stops each.

"The two remaining parcels in Oklahoma and Texas we should do together to give everyone a feeling for how it works."

"Whoa, this is going to be fun," said Sandra.

"Okay," Caroline said with sudden enthusiasm, "when do we start?"

CHAPTER 22

Leave No Trace Behind

"I forgot to mention one thing," Austin said as the six of them prepared for the initial run to Muskogee, "I didn't ask anyone's permission to bury parcels where I did, nor did I tell anyone what I did except C. Monica. Most are buried in wooded areas but still not always on public land. We can't just walk in and start digging whenever we want. We have to wait for nightfall or a time when no one's around to take notice. Even then, we have to be quiet, work quickly, and leave no trace behind."

"Good to know," said Juliana. "Getting arrested is not on my list of things to do."

"Been there," David said dryly. "Not fun."

"Not on my list, either," Caroline added. "It would set a bad example for my children."

Sandra and Rory laughed. So did Caroline, for what seemed like the first time in years.

"So, this isn't a test run; it's the real thing," Austin went on. "At the end of the night, we'll have in our possession one of the actual parcels."

They set off in early evening in three cars, paired up as Juliana had suggested, for the 140-mile drive to Muskogee. Austin had made sure they all had locator beacon software on their phones and had shown each how to use it. The entire family was eager to understand; not one was bored or disinterested. The secret mission, Sneaky Pete, pot of gold at the end of the rainbow aspect had everyone engaged.

"Do you use your navigation system everywhere, even when you know exactly where you're going?" Juliana asked once they were underway.

"Not to the grocery store but otherwise pretty much," Austin replied. "Map Lady keeps me on track if I get distracted."

"She gets a bit bossy at times," Juliana observed, "like when you

104

don't follow what she says and pull off the road for gas or lunch. She keeps telling you to turn around."

"I just turn her off, then start up again when I'm back on the road. She reconfigures the route based on where you are now, then give new directions. It happens fast."

"Sounds helpful," Juliana said.

"It is, especially in the dark or rain when you can't see well. But sometimes, just for a change, I'd like to have a version that makes smart-aleck remarks when I miss a turn or go some way other than she says."

"You mean like 'Watch where you're going, knucklehead,' or 'If you're not going to take my advice find your own way.'"

"Yeah," Austin replied, "just for entertainment."

"I can see traveling with you will be interesting."

"I hope so. We'll be on the road a week, maybe more."

"A week," Juliana said. "That could be a long, long trip if we don't get along."

"I'm a friendly sort," Austin countered.

"We'll mark that down as a good start."

The three-car convoy pulled into Muskogee and was soon cruising down Batfish Road past War Memorial Park on the town's north side. Everyone slowed and parked in a dark roadway following Austin's lead.

"This is home to the actual submarine USS Batfish," Austin said to the group. "It sank three enemy subs in 76 hours during World War II, which set a record of some kind. These grounds are a memorial to all submarines lost in the war.

"And since we've now had our history lesson, Parcel Twelve is buried over there in those trees," he said, pointing. "Bring up the beacon app on your phones and see what you get."

"I see a blinking red dot," said Caroline.

"So do I," said Rory. The others were all nodding.

"War Memorial Park is only open on weekends and I don't see anyone around," Austin said. "It's a clear, starry night so we have no problem with the weather. Just walk casually, letting the phone lead you toward the dot. I'll bring the shovel."

They walked slowly, staring at their phones until they entered the group of trees Austin had pointed out. Sandra's phone started beeping, then David's, then everyone's, and soon all six phones held a steady dot and beep overtop a blank spot of dirt.

"Looks like we've found it," Juliana said. "who wants to dig?"

105

"I will," said Rory, eager to do his part. Austin spread out his tarp.

"Okay, here's the shovel, but be sure to put the dirt on this tarp and not toss it all over."

Before long, Rory had dug down to a buried object. David took over to clear enough dirt away to pull it out.

"Wow, this is it," Sandra said. Juliana and Caroline took turns filling the hole and soon only a slight indentation showed.

"Looks good," Austin said, "let's go back to the cars."

Once there, David removed the outer protective bag, unclamped the plastic tub's lid, and pulled it off to reveal the authentic Parcel Twelve, also in a protective bag.

"So, this is our buried treasure," he said. "With all this packaging you used, it would probably be safe for a hundred years."

"One down," Caroline said, "16 to go. This project might not be so difficult after all."

"Maybe not," said Austin.

"I was thinking there's no need for us all to go to the stop in Texas," David said. "Rory and I will be headed east and can add it to our list if it's as easy as this one."

"It won't be, but I think you can manage it. Just remember, all of you, don't ever open a parcel. The opening comes at the end once you have all 17. If anyone breaks this rule, the whole deal is off.

"Oh, another thing I forgot to mention," Austin added. "There's a second way to find a parcel if the locator beacon doesn't work for some reason. In the Maps function on your phone, enter the GPS coordinates Sandra and Rory faithfully copied out onto the map. It will take you right to the location. The same procedure works in your car's navigation system."

A few of them tried it. The resulting screen showed a travel line going directly to the grove of trees where the parcel had been.

"Good to have a backup," Juliana said. "Is there anything else you 'forgot' to tell us?"

"Probably," Austin replied. "I'll let you know if I think of anything."

Then they got in the cars to head back home.

The entire unearthing had taken just over an hour. Not a single bicycle, car, or dog-walker had passed them. Maybe this would go easily, Austin thought. Maybe.

CHAPTER 23

A Bit Paranoid, Don't You Think?

Fully briefed on destinations and procedures and eager to hit the road, the adventurers piled into cars the morning of Monday, June 17. Rory and Sandra had prepared an envelope for each vehicle containing a copy of the overall map they'd drawn, Austin's original letters about specific parcels they were to find, and any associated keys or claim tickets. It would be a grand quest, and they were ready to go.

Caroline and Sandra headed off to Be-AT-rice, Nebraska, about a six-hour drive.

David and Rory were going to Smithville, Texas, just a half-hour longer.

In Austin's car, he and Juliana were on their way to Rapid City, South Dakota, a 13-hour drive that would put them there in late evening.

"I never asked anyone what his or her capacity was for road trips," Austin said as he drove.

"Another one of those things you 'forgot?'"

"Yeah, one of those. Can you keep going all day or do you have some limit like 250 miles or six hours or something?"

"With two drivers I can go all day and night," Juliana replied. "On my own, five or six hundred miles is enough. After that I get tired and start to fall asleep. Since you've done all this mileage before and drive for a living, I suspect you're the Mad Max Road Warrior type."

"Sometimes, if I'm on deadline," Austin replied, "but I don't focus obsessively on the destination like I once did. I try to see what I see along the way."

"How did you ever get a job going around the county hiding things?"

"Someone recommended me, I think."

"You and how many others?"

"I don't know if there were other applicants or not. I didn't see or hear about anyone else interviewing. Maybe I was the only one who believed such a job could exist. Anyway, I walked in, met C. Monica, answered her questions, and she answered mine. I got hired and received a big payment in advance. It was almost enough to make me suspicious."

"How so?"

"Like, why was this so easy? Why was I being paid so much? Was I being set up for something?"

"Set up for what?" Juliana asked.

"Well, maybe these parcels are stuffed with rocks and newspaper, and I'm just a handy person to blame for stealing whatever was supposed to be in them."

"Or maybe," Juliana said, joining in, "this whole treasure hunt is an elaborate MacGuffin, like The Maltese Falcon, and the real mission is something or somebody or somewhere else?"

"Yeah, maybe."

"A bit paranoid, don't you think?"

"Probably, but it crossed my mind a time or two driving around the country."

"I'm sure you're safe there. Dad wouldn't do such a thing to anyone and neither would any of us."

"I wish I'd met your dad," Austin continued after a period of silence. "Talking with him might have helped form a picture of what this whole business is about. It sure is a puzzling thing."

"He was good to us when we were kids but drifted away as we got older. He gradually receded into his business world after mom died and didn't take much interest in family.

"But then something changed," she went on. "He wasn't always busy anymore. He started traveling the world and even took us along. We were puzzled why this happened so all of a sudden, but we did have a great time visiting other countries."

"Where did you go?"

"We each spent two months traveling with him," she replied and then went on to tell of places they'd all seen.

"Then came the huge surprise," she went on; "he got us interested in owning and operating the ice cream shop."

"The Board Room?" Austin said. "Where people go for Monopoly tournaments?"

"The very one."

"I've played in those but never won very often. I like it because it's open to anyone. I've played against 80-year-olds and fourth graders and all the while ate tons of ice cream and hot dogs and chips. It's a great place."

"We wondered about the idea at first but everyone joined in and it became a major success. I think it's what this parcel-recovery, treasure-hunt, grand expedition we're on is all about – getting everyone to pitch in and work together."

"It seems to be working," said Austin.

"I suppose it is," Juliana replied. "I expected enthusiasm for The Board Room to wear off after a year or so but it hasn't. Everyone is still having fun."

Austin veered from Map Lady directions in the northern part of Kansas to take US Route 281 to the town of Lebanon. He continued a couple of miles past it, turned left on Kansas Highway 191, and soon pulled to a stop at a tiny white building in what seemed to be a small park. Juliana looked puzzled.

"Are we somewhere?" she asked.

"We're at the very geographic center of the 48 United States. It's a somewhere in the middle of nowhere."

They got out and walked around. The site had a welcoming sign, a monument and plaque giving geographic location details, a covered picnic pavilion, and the small white chapel which had space for eight people.

"Why are we here?" Juliana asked.

"It's one of those happened-to-be-in-the-neighborhood things, something fun to visit just because we're close by."

"Okay then, I'm here in the very middle of things. I should be perfectly balanced." She stood on one foot and leaned to one side, then the other. "I'm getting a message," she went on. "The Universe is telling me a picnic would be good. Too bad we didn't bring one."

They returned to the car and set off to find lunch on the way to Rapid City.

Behind them in Nebraska Caroline and Sandra were nearing their destination. They were headed to a campground, according to map notes, but had no gear or camping experience. It was just as well. It was a blistering hot day and sleeping in a tent would have been miserable. Also, they weren't outdoor, sleep on the ground, survive in the wilderness types. They decided to work out how to retrieve the parcel when they got closer.

Chautauqua Park Campground was on the south side of Beatrice some distance from the city itself. Caroline drove around the area a while just to see what was there.

"I got it," Sandra said suddenly. She was looking at her phone. "Keep driving the way you're going and I'll direct you." Caroline drove, turned, and finally stopped when Sandra said to.

"It's over there in those trees," Sandra said, "just a few hundred feet from here."

"Okay, let's think about this," replied Caroline. "This is a campground. It's the middle of the afternoon and hardly anyone's here. If we wait till dark more people will come. How about we load the folding shovel in your pack and go for an afternoon stroll like we're watching birds or looking for flowers or mushrooms or something."

"Great idea, Mom," Sandra said and they soon began moseying along as if they had nothing else to do but enjoy the afternoon.

"In here," said Sandra. They looked around, saw no one, then turned into the trees. Soon Sandra's phone hovered with a steady dot and beep over a blank spot on the ground.

"I'll start," Caroline said, "and we can take turns."

They spread out a tarp as Austin had shown them and began. When they'd dug a foot or so down three dogs suddenly invaded, all small and sniffing and running around yapping at everything. Their owner, a tiny gray-haired woman, tried to calm them.

"Max, Trixie, Luigi, stop it!" she said. "Stop barking! Stop making so much noise!" Her commands made no difference as the dogs continued to race around and bark. Finally, the woman walked through the brush to where they were digging.

"What are you doing here?" she demanded. "Why are you digging? Does management know about this? Do you have permission to be here?"

"We're looking for something put here long ago," Caroline said as dogs continuously barked in their annoying yappy dog voices. "We'll only be a few minutes, and then we'll be gone."

"Whatever you dig up belongs to the campground because it's on their property. I will call and tell whoever's in charge what you're doing. We'll see what they think about this."

Sandra had found C. Monica's business card and called her on the phone.

"A little old lady with dogs is harassing us," Sandra told her. "Can you help us? We're trying to retrieve Parcel Three."

Sandra listened a moment, then handed the phone to the grey-haired woman. "It's the Attorney General," Sandra lied, "she wants to talk to you."

"Attorney General? Talk to me? What for? Have I done something wrong?" Sandra held out her phone without responding.

The woman took the phone and said hello, then listened … and listened … and continued to listen as seconds and then minutes went by.

"Oh," she finally said, "I'm sorry if I was being a problem. It won't be necessary to send arresting officers. It's just my little dogs; they get so enthusiastic." She handed the phone back to Sandra. "The person I talked to told me I could be detained and questioned for interference and should leave at once," she said. "I'm perplexed about what you're doing here but I guess it's none of my business."

She walked back through the bushes calling her dogs to her. Max, Trixie, and Luigi were still barking but finally left.

"Attorney General?" C. Monica said to Sandra. "Where'd you get such an idea?"

"I just made it up."

"Pretty funny, but I suggest you finish up quickly and get moving before anyone has a chance to think about what happened." They were both laughing when Sandra disconnected.

Moving swiftly, they retrieved the plastic tub from the earth. Sandra stuffed it in her pack, they refilled the hole, then walked to the car no longer in a carefree manner.

"Ta-da, Parcel Three, just as advertised," Sandra said after she removed the outer plastic bag and lid from the tub. "Aren't we just doing great?"

"Let's go to town," said Caroline. "I'm hungry. There's sure to be a burger or pizza place somewhere."

They stopped to mail the parcel in the box they'd been provided, then found a place to have pizza. In a motel room later, Caroline called Becky to report their location and progress for the day.

"Pretty easy going," Sandra said later, "if you just ignore having to threaten a busybody little old lady and her yappy dogs."

"It was rather fun," Caroline replied. "Good thinking about calling C. Monica. Attorney General – so great. It added just enough drama to make this a real adventure."

"My mother wants *drama*," Sandra said with a shocked expression. "Who would have ever suspected?"

CHAPTER 24

It's a Potato Chip, You Moron

Rory had entered Parcel Thirteen's GPS coordinates in the navigation system and now Map Lady was directing them to it.

"Looks like it leads to a lake," he said.

"The edge of one I hope," said David, "not the middle."

"Yeah, on the south shore of it, but the burial spot isn't near any roads. It looks like we might have to hike overland a while."

"Is there anything in your map notes about it?"

Rory unfolded the map and consulted it for a moment.

"Oh, right, this is where Austin rented the canoe. How are you on canoes?"

"I can row a boat as long as you don't want to go in a straight line," David replied. "I just meander all over. The truth of it is I don't like being in boats much at all."

"I don't like boats, either, and paddling a canoe is way different. I'll see if I can find a park map." Rory was quiet while he searched the Internet on his phone.

"We'll be there in a couple of hours," David said. "Maybe we can get this done today."

"Success means a steak dinner, right?" Rory said in a hopeful tone.

"It's as good a reason as any."

Grandpa Xander was a different sort of person, Rory was thinking. He'd worked something close to magic or voodoo with his investments and always seemed mysterious and unapproachable. The thought of traveling with him was almost scary. But Rory and Sandra ended up having a great time in Mexico and South America and now thought their grandpa was super cool. They were sad he had died.

His death set off this parcel project which Rory found odd. Why go to all this trouble? Wouldn't an ordinary will do the job? He wondered what grandpa had been thinking, why he'd made this process so involved.

But it was fun. Here Rory was, on the road helping solve a mystery, and solving something was fun.

David was driving, following Map Lady's directions, and making good time.

"The Board Room's been in business seven years now," Rory said, "and every day new people come in and are surprised to find us there like we just opened or something."

"Same thing happens when I'm on shift," David said.

"I first thought having a big room with tables to play Monopoly was kind of strange," Rory continued, "but they're full nearly every day and we sell tons of food and ice cream to the players. The Bunker downstairs is totally outrageous. People even dress up to match the version of Monopoly they're playing."

"Potato chips were a great idea, part of dad's original plan, as I recall. People start eating them and keep ordering because they can't stop. Having several different kinds of chips helps sell even more."

"Exactly how it goes," said Rory. "We run out of one kind or another nearly every day. We don't order large quantities because people are nuts about everything being fresh. Is it fresh, they ask? I keep wanting to say: 'It's a potato chip, you moron. We got them in this morning. If it's not green or rubbery, it's fresh.'"

David drove into Buescher State Park and took the loop road around the lake.

"Any red dots yet?" he asked.

"Not yet, but the park map I found shows a stream on the south side. I'm pretty sure Austin buried it somewhere near there. When you see a road leading to a playground or recreation hall, turn and follow it to the end. We'll be maybe a quarter-mile away and can walk to it without needing a canoe.

"It's just as well," David said. "The weather's starting to look pretty nasty for canoes."

He found the turnoff and drove to a parking area at the end. There was no one in the playground and nothing going on in the recreation building.

"I'm getting a blinking dot now," Rory said.

They left the car and followed the phone map toward the lake. When they came to the stream Rory had mentioned, they couldn't tell which direction water flowed because it had flooded and overflowed its banks.

"We'll have to wade pretty soon if we keep going this direction," David said.

"Guess so," Rory replied, "but it's exactly where the map is leading us."

They entered a wooded area and were soon in water to their knees. Both their phones showed a steady dot and beep.

"Here it is," David said, "in two feet of water. I wonder if Austin's Coat of Many Colors included a wetsuit."

Rory started digging. Every shovel full of dirt became mud as he removed it, and water immediately flowed in to take its place.

Progress was slow.

Rory kept digging.

David took over after a time but it seemed like they were getting nowhere.

"It's like shoveling water into a grocery cart," Rory said.

"We're half a shovel length down, maybe two feet," David replied. "Only one more to go."

It was starting to rain. They kept digging mud from a hole full of water. Finally, after more than an hour of it, and now in pouring rain, Rory felt the shovel hit something solid.

"Found it," he said. "Now we have to clear enough space to get hold of it." He kept digging, bringing up shovels full of mud he threw in any direction. Piling dirt on the tarp would be useless here.

Finally, he got down on his knees and plunged his whole upper torso, arms extended, into the hole. After a considerable struggle and rooting around, he emerged with the packaged parcel.

"Steak dinner it is," he gasped, water and mud running down his face.

Making no attempt to refill the hole, they waded to dry land, then walked back to the car where David removed the parcel's outer packaging. It was full of water but the plastic tub inside it had held: Parcel Thirteen was completely dry. David put it in a mailing box to take to town.

"This certainly didn't go as easy as the test run to Muskogee," David said, "but we emerged victorious nonetheless. Now we shower, change clothes, find a laundry, and head for our steak dinner. We're in Texas so we'll find steakhouses everywhere. Pick one you like but make sure it has a bar."

"I don't hang out in bars," Rory said, "but it would seem odd to find a steakhouse without one."

Austin pulled up to the Rapid City bus station late in the evening. They'd stopped for an early dinner at Wall Drug, mainly because they couldn't just drive by an attraction with unrelenting road signs starting 650 miles away, and thus found the bus station had closed at 6:00 PM.

"Oops," Austin said, "I wasn't paying attention. I should have remembered."

"It's not like we're in any hurry," Juliana said. "Let's go back to Wall Drug and look around some more. Maybe we could buy stuff. You have to have stuff, you know."

"Okay, and you can drop me at a campground and pick me up in the morning for breakfast. There's no need to be early; the bus station doesn't open until 11:00."

"You sure? I have a ton of expense money; I can get you a motel room. You could even share mine."

"I brought my gear, and it's nice out," Austin said. "I'll be fine."

"Then let's get something else to eat first," Juliana said. "I'm hungry again."

"Are we talking healthy food here, like some sprout restaurant that's a two-acre salad bar?"

"This is a road trip; I get healthy food at home. No, tonight it's a thick chocolate shake, maybe even French fries. I wouldn't rule out a margarita either."

"Fabulous idea," Austin said. "I'm all over it like pink rubber bands on your little sister's braces."

"But I'm the little sister," Juliana replied with a laugh, "and I never had braces. Did I miss out on something?"

She dropped him later at the Sleepy Hollow Campground and returned in the morning. They went to breakfast, did more tourist wandering, then arrived again at the bus station just after it opened.

"I'll go get it," Juliana said. She took the locker key from the package Rory and Sandra had given them and returned with the tub containing Parcel Seven a few minutes later.

"Too easy," she said. "All this whoop-de-whoop about finding a mysterious hidden object and it takes two minutes?"

"It did take us a while to get here," said Austin. "You should probably say two days and two minutes."

"Where to next?" Juliana asked.

"Billings, Montana, a little over five hours from here."

After mailing the parcel to C. Monica and making the update call to Becky, they were on their way.

CHAPTER 25

I Checked Your Record

Caroline and Sandra arrived in Wichita, Kansas, in early afternoon. Their destination, The Old Cowtown Museum, was on the bank of the Arkansas River near the center of town. Sandra drove slowly through an area called Museums on the River, discovered a botanical garden, a golf course, an art museum, an All-Indian Center, and then pulled into the Cowtown Museum parking lot.

"Looks kind of busy right now," she said. Several people were sitting in chairs on the Visitor Center front porch.

"I'm showing a blinking dot on my phone map," replied Caroline. "We're close, but there are too many people here to dig it up now. Let's see what Cowtown is about, then head into the city and come back when it's dark."

They paid their admission and walked the museum's boardwalk and dirt paths through the town. They watched a Blacksmith hammer out a horseshoe, perused items in a furniture store, ate a hot dog at Fritz Snitzler's Saloon, read old advertising signs posted in store windows, all to pass the time while they and a few dozen other visitors waited for the next scheduled gunfight to take place in the town's wide main street. They enjoyed costumed cowboys and ranchers play out their parts – which included shooting each other – then laughed and applauded at its conclusion when the bowler-hatted town doctor pronounced most of the participants dead and frisked them for cash in the process.

Then Sandra did a brief search on her phone.

"There's a Dillard's store in Wichita. Let's go shopping and get you a couple more dresses and more shoes. You can never have too many shoes."

"So I'm finding out," Caroline replied. "All I need is a good reason to wear them."

"It probably won't be here in an 1865 cowboy town," Sandra

116

observed, "but I'll bet we can find a few high-class restaurants where you could try them out. After all, what good is expense money if you don't have expenses?"

Rory was driving east on I-10 heading for the Golden Nugget Hotel and Casino in Biloxi, Mississippi. It didn't matter what time they got there since the casino was open all day and night. They stopped for lunch in Beaumont, Texas, after making their way through Houston, and now in mid-afternoon were cruising through Louisiana. It was a watery route over rivers, bayous, and swamps. There were occasional views south to bays and lakes and then into Mississippi Sound and the Gulf of Mexico.

"I called Becky at our lunch stop," David said. "She said Caroline and Juliana both found their parcels, which means we've collected four of them and it's only our second day on the road."

"Maybe we'll have them all by the end of the week," Rory replied. "Then we only have to drive home. How's Becky doing, by the way?"

"Chipper, as always, working nearly every day at The Board Room to keep it running. The Monopoly playing tables have been busy all week, she said. A big group drove a hundred miles from Tulsa yesterday just to play all day, and another group is in from Lawton today. They're eating their way through the inventory, hot dogs and ice cream disappearing fast. She's run out of potato chips every day and had to call in double orders."

"Is she bothered because we're gone for a week and she has to get around by herself?"

"Not at all, but she does like getting our calls."

"I'm sure it's good to know how we're doing," Rory said.

They pulled into the Golden Nugget in early evening and decided to eat in the dining room. There were several casino restaurants to choose from, offering everything from steak to seafood to Asian to sports bar pub food. They couldn't pass up the Bubba Gump Shrimp Company, however, and there loaded up on local fare.

David took the lockbox claim ticket to the Cashier afterward.

"This has been here for three years," the Cashier said in surprise after searching casino records.

"Uh-huh," David replied, "I forgot about it."

"Just a minute, I'll check with my manager." He did so and reported back. "There's an additional $500 charge, sir."

"Would buying $500 worth of chips work?" David asked. The Cashier talked on the phone some more.

"Yes, it would," he finally said.

David paid in $100 bills, took the lockbox key and the chips and soon had Parcel Two under his arm. He located Rory.

"Put this in the car would you, please?" he said.

"Better yet," Rory replied, "I'll box it up and mail it since it's all prepaid. I'll be right back."

"Great, then come join me; we have some gambling to do."

Wonderful, Rory was thinking. Gambling, cheap drinks, no closing time, frequent encouraging whoops of joy when people won something; what could go wrong?

David's first $500 worth of chips disappeared in five minutes. Whatever life skills he had, Blackjack, Poker, and Roulette weren't among them. But with low-priced drinks readily at hand he appeared not to be discouraged. The second $500 went more slowly, and by mid-way through the third $500 he was winning. Intermittently, of course, but winning.

He was about $250 short of breaking even when Rory convinced him to leave. David was on his seventh Whiskey Sour by then and his decision-making, along with his navigation, was getting a bit woozy. They paid the bill and made their way to the car.

"But I was winning," David protested. "I was winning."

"Which is an excellent time to leave," Rory said. "We found the parcel, you won back half the $500 storage charge, you had a bunch of drinks, and now it's two o'clock in the morning. You were sure to start losing again soon."

"I didn't much care whether I won or lost. It was just fun to be there doing something I've never done."

"Meanwhile, we have nearly 900 miles to go to our next stop," Rory said once they'd settled in the car. "Should we get some done yet tonight?" But David was already asleep.

"Sounds like a Yes to me," Rory said and he and Map Lady headed east.

A police car pulled them over before he'd driven three miles.

"Hello," Rory said when the officer came to his window.

"May I see your license and registration, please?" Rory got his license from his wallet and the car's registration from behind the overhead sunshade.

118

"Please wait here," said the officer and took license and registration back to her vehicle.

"What's happening?" David asked, waking up.

"Cops pulled me over."

"Did they say why?"

"Not yet."

The officer returned after what seemed like a long time.

"Your name is Rory Michael Griffith, and you're 18 years old, according to your license, correct?"

"Yes."

"But this is not your car. It's registered to a Mr. David Moorhouse."

"I'm David," David said. "It's my car, and I'm Rory's uncle."

"You just came from the Golden Nugget Casino?"

"We did," Rory answered.

"You are aware the legal age for gambling in Mississippi is 21?"

"I just went in for dinner. Uncle David was doing the gambling."

"I see," the officer said, "a customer's age is not a police matter; it's for the casino to manage." She now directed her questions to David. "Were you drinking while you gambled?"

"I was, which is why Rory is driving."

"Very wise. I checked your record and found you have multiple arrests for possession of drugs."

"True, sad to say, but it wasn't for selling them; it was just for smoking weed."

"Do you have drugs with you in the car now?"

"No, we don't," David answered. Another police vehicle arrived just then.

"I'd like you both to step out of the vehicle while we check."

David and Rory got out and the second officer and her K9 dog searched the car. They found nothing.

"Looks like you're clear," the first officer said, "but we also got a report from a casino patron suggesting you, Mr. Griffith, might have been kidnapped by the person you're with and were there against your will. Since you were driving when I stopped you, and you haven't indicated you're in any danger, I'll disregard it unless you know some reason I shouldn't."

"No, I'm fine," Rory said. "It's just my uncle and me driving to North Carolina."

"Very well," the officer said. "You can be on your way. Drive safely."

119

Rory pulled back onto the road and continued to Greenville, North Carolina.

"Well, wasn't that entertaining," David said.

"I wasn't sure what to say or do," Rory said, "but I figured answering her questions politely and telling the truth was the best plan."

"Excellent choice, Rory. One thing I've learned watching too much TV is never, ever say 'I wasn't doing anything wrong.' It's a sure sign you were and you know it.

"By the way, I'm really, really glad you got Parcel Two mailed off. It might have been a problem if they'd wanted to open it. We might have had to play the C. Monica card at way too early in the morning."

Caroline and Sandra had been at the Old Cowtown Museum while this was going on. They'd kept busy in Wichita for many hours (resulting in several new packages in the car's back seat) and had indeed gone to an upscale restaurant, both wearing classy new outfits.

Back at the museum site, they now proceeded with flashlights and shovel in hand, a blinking dot on the map, and increasingly insistent beeping from Sandra's phone. They climbed the embankment to the right of the Visitor Center to a spot just beyond its crest. They dug out dirt and shoveled it onto the tarp, retrieved Parcel Fourteen and refilled the hole, then crept silently back to the car.

"This is fun, Mom," Sandra said.

"It kind of is," Caroline replied. "Maybe we should do this more often?" They both laughed and drove off to their lodgings for the night.

Austin and Juliana were in a cemetery in Billings, Montana. They also had waited till dark to make their way to the appointed spot, dig a hole, and retrieve the parcel.

"You sure you don't want to put your tent up here?" Juliana said as she put Parcel Ten in its box for mailing.

"Not here. Some kind of Cemetery Watch Squad sent me packing when I was here to bury this thing. We need to be gone before they show up. Also, it smells like it's soon going to rain. I think I'll accept your offer of a motel room."

"Okay, but you're missing an opportunity," she teased. "When the sun rises tomorrow, you could say 'It's Resurrection Morning, and I'm the first one up.'"

CHAPTER 26

An Oblong Shape in the Distance

Juliana was driving, following directions to the ghost town near Jackpot, Nevada. The route led southwest through Montana, across a corner of Wyoming, down into eastern Idaho, and over the Nevada border to Jackpot, then farther south and finally onto a dirt road leading west. They'd been driving non-stop all day. Finally, about six o'clock in the evening, they arrived at the old mill site Austin remembered.

Something was wrong.

GPS coordinates from the map pointed to a flat, leveled area that wasn't there when he'd been here before. Standing on it, Austin got no response from the parcel's beacon.

"Problem?" Juliana asked.

"I buried the parcel right here where I'm standing," he replied, "but it wasn't graded flat like this. There was a rocky mound here."

"So, someone was here with a bulldozer?"

"Yeah, I guess, and it looks like it wasn't recently. Someone smoothed out this area for some purpose, then abandoned the idea and never came back. But regardless, were the parcel still here we'd be seeing a dot on the map."

"Let's walk around and see if it shows up," Juliana said. They did so in widening circles, but the farther they went, the more silent and unresponsive the evening became.

"Let's each go a different direction and range out farther," Austin said.

They walked in zig-zag patterns, Juliana west and Austin east, straying farther and farther from the car. The sun was headed for the horizon and would set around eight o'clock, so they still had a couple of hours before they'd have to continue the following day.

"Not finding anything," Juliana shouted. There was no response. She kept going, zig-zagging east.

Austin hadn't heard her. He stopped, looked around in waning daylight and wished he'd brought a flashlight.

Then Juliana got a faint, intermittent glimmer of a dot. It grew stronger as she continued, then began to blink dimly on the map about a half-mile away. She tried to phone Austin but the signal was too weak, so she sent a text message instead – *found something, drive west with lights on* – thinking the phone would keep trying to send as signal fluctuated up and down.

Austin got the message almost right away but where was the car? He turned about and began walking back, holding the car key fob out ahead of him. Soon the horn honked and lights came on so he jogged the remaining distance. He got in, drove west, and before long spotted a waving figure in the distance.

"There's a dot barely showing about a half-mile over there," she said, pointing. "Drive as far as the car can make it."

The terrain grew steep and rocky in a quarter-mile so they left headlights shining and went on foot. Beeping from the phone grew stronger as they advanced.

"There's something," Juliana said, pointing to an oblong shape in the distance. They went toward it and found a familiar plastic tub in a pile of rocks. Its outer protective bag was gone. The cover showed teeth marks, but whatever chewed on it did not get it open. Parcel Sixteen and its locator beacon were still safe inside.

"How did it ever get here?" Juliana wondered. "We must be nearly a mile from the old mill."

"Just guessing, but the dozer must have left it partly buried in the flattened-out area," Austin said. "Then something, most likely coyotes, found it and dragged it around and eventually left it here."

"I suppose they lost interest when it didn't smell like food or when chewing on the lid didn't get it open," Juliana filled in. "Which means it's been sitting unprotected out here in open desert for any number of years but we still found it."

"*You* found it, actually," Austin said. "This is great; I was getting concerned."

"Let's get back to town while we can still find the way." She turned the car around and headed overland toward the black shape of the old mill they could still see in the distance, then got on the dirt road and headed to Jackpot for the night.

The Mexican restaurant was closed so they had dinner in a steak and seafood place in the local casino.

"How are you on gambling?" Juliana asked.

"I'd like to win something big, for sure, but when it comes down to the actual moment of putting my money on the table, I can't do it. I worked for it. I don't want to lose it, especially since the odds are against me."

"I'm the same way but there's nothing much else to do here in a town of 1,200 people. Let's try our luck for a little while."

They played Blackjack. With nothing but rudimentary knowledge of the game, Austin consistently lost. Juliana won a couple rounds, lost several more, then started winning. Hand after hand her stack of chips grew. After about an hour, she signaled to quit for the night and cashed out.

"I won $4,300," she said.

"Wow, that's great!"

"The dealer started looking at me oddly; I thought it was time to leave."

"Probably the right thing to do," Austin said. "So, it's off to our rooms?"

"I have a room."

"One?" Austin said hesitantly.

"Yeah, imagine that."

Rory drove till early morning. They stopped for breakfast in Montgomery, Alabama, then David, now finally awake, drove through Georgia and South Carolina while Rory slept, then on to Greenville, North Carolina, by mid-afternoon.

They located the abandoned factory and activated the locator beacon as they drove by.

"It's here," Rory said. David parked and they went on an exploratory walk. The phone map led them to a spot along the railroad tracks just as Rory had read in the map notes. "Let's get the shovel and get this done now," he said.

They walked back to the car and saw a police vehicle parked next to it with its red and blue lights flashing.

"Uh-oh," Rory said, "what is it with you and police? Do they just like you?"

"They must. Let's find out what the officer wants," said David.

"I know about chick magnets, which can sometimes be great, but being a police magnet must be a real bummer."

They walked to the car, making no effort to stay out of sight, and greeted the officer.

"This is private property, sir," the officer said. "I was wondering why you were parked here. There have been several reports of vandalism recently."

"Someone won an award for a photo of this old factory," David said. "We were looking to see where the picture had been taken and possibly set up to take a few other pictures."

"Do you have permission from the property owners?"

"No, we don't. I saw a No Trespassing sign or two but nothing about not taking pictures. We didn't go inside the building."

"I suggest you get something in writing from the owner. We check this building every day. If you have authorization, you won't be bothered." The officer said goodbye and drove off.

"Did you just make the part up about the picture getting an award?" Rory asked. "It sounded like baloney to me. Plus, we don't even have a camera except on our phones."

"The award part is true," David replied. "I found it on the Internet."

"I'm impressed."

"And everyone thinks I'm useless."

"What do we do now?" Rory asked.

"Since we didn't sleep well last night, let's get a place to stay and something to eat. What do you suppose is good around here?"

"Barbeque," Rory answered without hesitation. "We're in North Carolina and pork barbeque is sacred here."

"What should we do about the parcel?" David asked later over a plateful of ribs.

"Here's a plan," Rory answered. "Drop me off there about three in the morning, then go park in a lot somewhere next to other cars. I'll go to where the parcel's buried, dig it up, then get out of sight somewhere close. I'll text you then to pick me up."

"Getting up at three in the morning isn't my usual thing," David said.

"Mine either but you probably won't magnetically attract police cars so early."

David dropped Rory off at the factory at the appointed time, then drove to an all-night McDonalds and parked. It was pouring rain. David watched through his rain-streaked windshield marveling at how many people bought burgers and fries in the rain at three in the morning. He idly wondered if The Board Room should be open late at night.

Rory, meanwhile, was out in the rain digging a hole. It was dark and quiet in the vicinity, no cars going by, no police cars going by, no people

124

in raincoats walking dogs going by. He retrieved Parcel Four and neatly refilled the hole. After folding up the tarp, he walked several blocks to a building with an overhanging awning, then texted his location to David.

"On my way," said David's text in return. Rory had been one of those who thought David might be essentially useless but he'd been valuable so far on this mission. Not big on leading the way but pretty good at doing the work.

David soon arrived. They returned to the motel and slept till mid-morning.

Mission accomplished.

Around noon, Sandra and Caroline pulled into Santa Fe, New Mexico, and headed directly to the pawnshop.

"Do you suppose I should put on a dress and give them my sweetest innocent look when I pick this up?" Sandra asked as Caroline parked outside it.

"Wouldn't hurt."

She changed into a short yellow dress in the back seat then got out to redeem the ticket.

"Wait a minute," Caroline said, "you can't go in wearing flip-flops. Find something a little more upscale, would you please?"

"Heels, Mom? Really?"

"You're the one who wanted to look sweet and innocent, and you made me wear heels to the lawyer's office."

Sandra rummaged through her luggage, found her one traveling pair and put them on.

"Better?" she asked.

"Very much."

Sandra went inside. The clerk looked at the ticket, looked at his records, looked up and down at Sandra, and said:

"This was left here ten years ago. What were you, four?"

"I was six. My dad left it here back then. Then he ran off, leaving my mom and me and my big brother. We just found the ticket and have been wondering what it was. Could I get it from you, please?"

"Oh, sorry, tough break for a young kid," said the man, "I'll get it right away if it's still here." Sandra already knew it was because the phone map had told her.

He returned ten minutes later with a very dusty package.

"Here you go," he said. "It was at the very bottom of a pile. Ordinarily, I'd have to charge you about $1,000 for it being here so long, but for

125

such a sweet young lady, I'll settle for $100." Sandra charged Caroline's credit card and left the shop, her heels making satisfying clicks on the floor.

They opened the tub inside the car.

"Hello, Parcel Eleven," Caroline said.

"I saved you $900 by dressing up," Sandra said.

"Totally worth it," her mother replied.

CHAPTER 27

No, and You Can't Make Me

C. Monica Stansbury sat at her desk and considered the latest development.

She'd been served weeks before with notice of suit for $250 million against the Xander Moorhouse Estate. The complainants were three individuals who'd purchased several of Moorhouse's more expensive properties. They were alleging fraud, misrepresentation, and failure to do one thing or another in a brazen effort to recover money which they, quite clearly, had agreed to and paid. They were opportunistically taking advantage of Moorhouse's death in an attempt to fleece estate heirs who were likely unschooled in complex financial matters.

Now, on her desk, was a request for a complete financial accounting of the Moorhouse Estate.

C. Monica did not have such an accounting.

Nobody did, and in this first formal test of Xander Moorhouse's revised financial strategy, nobody would.

Whether the heirs were familiar with the law or completely oblivious of it, the balance Moorhouse maintained on deposit fully paid and empowered C. Monica to protect their interests come what may.

Estate banking and investment accounts were entirely offshore.

Somewhere.

It could mean Cayman Islands, Switzerland, Belize, Germany – any of a half-dozen well-respected countries with advantageous structures and safeguards to keep money protected. Moorhouse had chosen one, C. Monica knew, and over many years had liquidated his assets and moved proceeds there.

But he'd never told her exactly where.

He didn't want her to know, and she didn't want to know.

Her firm didn't handle his financial matters and she preferred, for his protection, to keep it that way.

To withdraw money or even obtain a current balance required an identifying number for each account. C. Monica didn't have account numbers, nor did she know how many accounts there were, at which institutions, or even in what country. And further, access to accounts surely required passwords and likely other identification security. She certainly didn't have those.

These safeguards were what international banking was all about: protection from snoopers who tried to find out things none of their business. So even if the Grand Almighty IRS Itself demanded the information, presented sternly worded court orders, and showed up on-site with a half-dozen gorillas in matching black suits and curly wires in their ears, foreign country banks were entirely within their rights and their country's applicable laws to refuse.

Thus, finding Xander Moorhouse's assets and preparing an accounting thereof wasn't going to happen and C. Monica was formulating a response to say so. It would be multiple pages of legal boilerplate and procedural huff-and-puff, citing precedents and regulations and court cases, and exercising many well-worn tools in her arsenal of professional gambits, all of which would boil down to No, and you can't make me.

She didn't know whether a list of specific foreign banks and account numbers even existed anywhere. Moorhouse wouldn't have taken them to his grave. More than likely, there was information about the accounts somewhere in those 17 parcels.

The heirs only had to find it.

C. Monica knew from Becky Moorhouse's daily progress reports they were well on their way to doing so. They'd gotten themselves organized. They'd enlisted the aid of Austin Somerfeld. They'd made a plan and were carrying it out.

After three days on the road the intrepid group had recovered ten parcels. By the weekend they'd have located them all and be on their way home. His children working together in this fashion was precisely what the senior Moorhouse had hoped for.

In the meantime, parcels found thus far arrived regularly at the Stansbury Law Firm Office. C. Monica stacked them in the conference room closet still in their mailing boxes and kept the closet door locked. Once all 17 were in hand, parcels would be removed from their multiple layers of containment and arranged in numbered order to await revelation of their contents.

It was a plan nearly 20 years in the making.

Now it was happening.

Sometime in the next few weeks, the three Moorhouse heirs would appear by invitation in C. Monica's office and she'd orchestrate the final step in this grand family drama: the fateful sequential opening.

C. Monica was ready to see how this played out.

The question was: were they?

Would there be anger, disbelief, joy, drama, relief, heartache, resentment, people throwing things and stomping around the room? Very likely some or all of it might take place.

Sydney Bridgewater had now worked for Stansbury Law Firm ten years and had become ever more indispensable and valued as time passed. Still, despite offers of advancement within the firm, she'd preferred to continue her role as a Computer Systems Analyst in charge of keeping computers running. Her responsibility included computers on all employees' desks, along with the modest mainframe used for accounting work and maintaining the client historical document archive.

It had taken most of her first year to write coding changes she'd initially identified and to solve obvious problems of keeping these changes undetectable to clients, relentlessly methodical accountants, the law firm's management, and other computer wizards they might someday hire to search out mysteriously disappearing funds. So, when she finally implemented her new code just before a monthly billing, she was pleased a week later to see the result: $21,392.45 paid clandestinely to her. Such deposits, sometimes more, sometimes less, had continued each month up to the present day.

She'd also since enhanced her enhancements. For example, she could now remotely change the line-item skimming percentage to be larger, smaller, or zero; increase or decrease the occurrence of bogus miscellaneous expense items; and adjust retainer service fees up or down. She'd seen more than $2 million slide effortlessly and invisibly into a selection of a dozen bank accounts in cities all over the USA. Her total haul, including proceeds from previous employers still coming in, was slowly approaching $10 million. It would be a worthy milestone.

Some might call her actions embezzling.

Some might crassly call it stealing.

But Sydney was a very crafty thief and to her way of thinking, her minor larceny affected only clients who had tons of money and didn't notice or care. It was their silent and unknowing acknowledgment of her brilliant ingenuity.

But now she sensed potential trouble. She'd detected hints of vague suspicion about her which were starting to spread.

Not for her lifestyle: she drove an unremarkable Prius, lived in a modest two-bedroom apartment in a mid-scale section of town, and never wore extravagantly expensive clothes to work. She owned expensive clothes, mind you, which she wore to upscale restaurants and occasional late-night visits to local clubs, but they weren't for her job in the law office. To be sure, a computer programmer didn't wear $1,200 five-inch Louboutins to work when others wore sneakers or flip-flops.

It wasn't even her collection of expensive fountain pens. She always used the same one at work, the one her grandfather had given her, which is what she told people when they asked.

But what people noted and commented upon was she was unexplainably unambitious.

Though she welcomed new responsibilities without complaint and effortlessly carried them out, she'd repeatedly declined promotions.

Junior lawyers at law firms notoriously strove for advancement and were often even aggressive and pushy about it. Many would trample over friends and enemies alike to get ahead, to attain the glorious and exalted post of Law Firm Partner. In truth, being a Partner carried ominous responsibility for the firm's financial condition and, if needed, paying a share of substantial losses. But that reality never seemed to dim their holy quest for glory.

Someone who stayed happily in the same job year after year just wasn't normal. True, Sydney had received steady pay increases, but who would be content being just a Computer Systems Analyst year after year. It sounded dull, routine, and ... suspicious.

So, people talked, speculated, and surmised. There must be a reason, they thought, and conjectured, and wondered about. Maybe she was ... and people being the nosy busybodies they often were, in the absence of something substantive to think about filled in that blank with postulations bordering on the absurd.

Which, of course, Sydney heard about.

And thought about.

And her thinking told her it was getting time to move on.

Her software modifications would continue to run when she'd gone just like similar alterations still running at other places she'd worked. Monthly deposits would continue. She could still modify them up or down remotely. And should they be discovered and deleted, her recently implemented Overwatch module would detect their absence and reinstall them.

Moving on was disappointing in a way, yet intriguing.

Work at Stansbury Law Firm was enjoyable and coworkers were friendly and appreciative. But this vague background of distrust, combined with the lure of possible new opportunity, began to appear as a chance to get her crafty brilliance revved up and churning again.

Also, the Moorhouse parcels were stacking up in C. Monica's conference room. Before long all 17 would be there. Was this a smash-and-grab opportunity?

Sydney's instinct firmly told her no, stay away. Her life could be altered dramatically for the worse if she showed too much interest. Yet she wondered what was in them, as indeed did everyone else.

It was tempting.

CHAPTER 28

Why Are We Headed for Tuba City?

Rory drove north from Greenville to Virginia Beach, Virginia, then to US Highway 13 to cross Chesapeake Bay on CBBT: the Chesapeake Bay Bridge-Tunnel. This structure, costing nearly $400 million to build, is 23 miles long to cross the vast expanse of open water. It has a mile of tunnels between 25 and 100 feet underwater leading to and across four artificial islands. The crossing takes half an hour. For some drivers, being out of sight of land in their car for many miles, or driving in underwater tunnels, can be claustrophobic and scary.

"Where are we going?" David asked, sounding alarmed.

"Across a bridge and through some tunnels," Rory answered.

"Are you sure this is the shortest way? I don't see anything but water."

"It might be the shortest, I didn't check, but you can't come this way and not drive it. It's some kind of engineering wonder. It's also fun."

"If you say so."

Drivers for hire can assist if a motorist prefers but Rory completed the passage safely and continued north, passing through a stretch of Maryland and then into Delaware.

"It says here we go to a beach," David said. "Is this a picnic?"

"It could be with some lunch and a blanket."

"There's the tarp we use for digging, so mark me down for Yes on lunch."

They drove past many beaches to find the correct one, then followed the locator beacon map to the appropriate remote section. The lunch idea had turned into spicy Italian spaghetti with meatballs and breadsticks to go, plus a six-pack of Stella Artois, and they spread it out on the tarp exactly where the dot was showing steady on the phone.

Rory focused first on spaghetti. It was still hot, and any digging would surely get sand in it.

It was a matter of priorities.

The meal was terrific, as was the beer.

He began to dig a deep hole a while later and the shovel soon bounced off something at the bottom. He widened the hole, retrieved the tub, shoveled sand back in and had another Stella.

A nap seemed like a good idea. Nobody bothered them; it was a Thursday afternoon on an overcast June day and hardly anyone was around.

Sounds of heavy equipment awakened them an hour later. A flatbed trailer backed onto position nearby preparing to offload a bulldozer. Two more trailers followed, then another, until the deserted beach was soon full of huge earthmoving equipment.

"What's this about?" Rory said as they packed up and headed to the car.

"Beats me," David replied. They gave it no further thought. At the car, Rory put Parcel Fifteen in its mailing box to send off on their way through town.

What it was "about" was explained in bold letters on a sign posted on a distant side of the beach. Construction for significant improvements was to begin the following Monday. There would be a new recreation facility including 20 beach cabanas. The existing sand would be dug out to a depth of six feet and eventually wholly replaced. In David's and Rory's carefree and oblivious lunching and napping and parcel retrieving, they had no idea that in three days, Parcel Fifteen would have been hauled away with tons of sand and lost forever.

Caroline drove I-40 west from Santa Fe to Albuquerque and Gallup, New Mexico, then across Arizona to Flagstaff. She turned north there for the short distance to Wupatki National Monument but at its marked visitor center turn-off, Map Lady said to continue north. Caroline followed as directed, thinking there might be a second entrance, but soon began to think something was wrong.

"Why are we headed for Tuba City?" she asked Sandra after driving half an hour. She'd seen the name on the last highway mileage sign.

"I don't know; I was half asleep. I'll check."

Sandra looked ahead on the navigation system to see where it thought it was going.

"Map Lady is taking us to Page, Arizona," she finally said, "about a hundred miles north of here. That isn't where this Wupatki place is supposed to be."

"How did that happen?" asked Caroline.

"Not a clue. I entered the GPS numbers when we left Santa Fe and we've been following the same route ever since."

"Try entering them again." Caroline pulled off the road and stopped. Sandra got out the overall map and re-entered the Parcel Seventeen coordinates she'd written on it.

"Make a U-turn now," Map Lady said and showed a new route pointing behind them.

"I guess she changed her mind," said Caroline.

"I must have entered the numbers wrong in Santa Fe," Sandra said. "She's pointing to the right place now. Good thing you noticed. We were on our way to the Arizona border, then into Utah."

On their return, Caroline caught a momentary glimpse of something darting across the road in front of her. There came a sudden, sickening thump, the car lurched as it ran over something and a tire blew, and an object long and bent clattered noisily behind. She brought the vehicle to a stop.

"What happened?" Sandra asked, wide-eyed.

"I hit something," Caroline replied, "but I have no idea what."

She drove onto the road shoulder and they got out to look. They found a massive dent in the left front fender along with a smashed headlight. There was no front bumper, and they had a shredded right rear tire.

"Do we have a spare?" Sandra asked.

"I think so," Caroline said, "but does either of us know how to change it?"

"I don't," Sandra said. "Rory would know and could help us figure it out."

Caroline looked off in the direction they'd been heading.

"I think we may have an even bigger problem," she said. "Look up ahead."

Far in the distance they saw many tiny dots on the road coming toward them. The dots got more prominent as they watched and soon resolved into the unmistakable shape of motorcycles.

"Oh, great," Sandra said, "two women alone on a deserted road and here comes a bunch of bikers."

"Looking on the bright side," Caroline replied, "I'll bet they know how to change a tire."

There was nothing to do but wait. The bikers came ever closer, stopped near them in a long line at the edge of the road, and soon

Caroline and Sandra were surrounded by 23 bearded or scruffy men in bandanas and leather jackets.

"Can we be of assistance?" one said. Another came forward with the tangled remains of the car's bumper.

"Looks like you lost this," he said.

"I hit something," was all Caroline could muster to say.

"Let's take a look," the first man said. He examined the fender dent and space where the bumper was missing, pulled something bristly from the casing around the broken headlight, and looked over the shredded tire and damaged bumper.

"You hit a pig," he said, "javelina, to be more specific. It left these bristly hairs behind along with its self-portrait in your fender. Hitting it knocked off your bumper, which shredded your tire when you ran it over."

"Where's the pig?" Caroline asked. "I thought I saw something run across the road in front of me but I don't see it anywhere now."

"Hitting it sent it flying into the brush beside the road, most likely. If you don't see it there, it probably got up and limped away. Mostly, I think you just ticked it off."

"Who are you guys?" Sandra timidly asked.

"Excuse me for not explaining to start with. We're guys from Flagstaff who like to ride our Harleys. I'm Leroy, a dentist. Jerry over there is an attorney, Craig is an off-duty cop, Franklin a house-painter, Wilson a surgeon, Grant sells insurance, and so forth. If you have a spare tire, I'm sure we can change it for you."

Caroline popped open the trunk. Two bikers changed the tire within just a few minutes and put the damaged bumper and tire in the trunk.

"Your car is mostly safe to drive," said Craig, the off-duty cop. "Just don't drive at night. You'll want to get a replacement tire when you're next in town and have the other damage repaired when you get back to Oklahoma. At least your license plate says Oklahoma is where you're from."

"We are," Caroline said, "and thank you all so much for your help."

"You are very welcome," Leroy said, and soon 23 motorcycles fired up and headed down the road.

"Guess you were right, Mom. They did know how to change a tire."

"And we hit a flying pig," said Caroline. "Won't that be a great story to tell."

They gingerly drove south, turned where the sign said to, and eventually parked near the Wupatki Visitor Center. The car's navigating map still pointed into the distance and the phone map showed a dot blinking in the same direction.

"It's telling us we have some hiking to do," Sandra said, "somewhere out in those rocks."

"Then let's suit up for hiking and become moseying tourists again."

The phone led them away from the main Wupatki ruins over rocky ground into a ravine where they were out of sight. As usual, they took turns digging.

"Something about this seems different," Caroline said. "The ground is looser than other places we've been digging and the surface seems more recently disturbed. It's almost like someone dug this one up already." Sandra did not comment.

But they eventually dug down to find a buried plastic tub that looked just like the others. Once they'd finished, it and the shovel went into Sandra's pack and they moseyed their way back to the car.

"Which parcel is this?" Caroline asked. "I've lost track."

"Seventeen," Sandra said, stripping off the outer packaging and popping the tub lid. "We now have only one to go."

"Excellent. Give Becky a call as soon as you get a phone signal. I'll take us back to Flagstaff to mail the parcel and get a new tire, though I'm pretty sure they'll want to replace all four. Then we'll find a delicious so-glad-to-be-alive dinner someplace."

Juliana drove north to Twin Falls, Idaho, then northwest on I-84 to Boise. They had a deadline today and wanted to be in place by noon. They stopped for lunch, then found their way to the Five Mile Gulch trailhead.

"I was here ten years ago in October," Austin said. "The scenery was fabulous and I hiked in and stayed overnight. Now it's mid-June and everything will look wonderful in a different way."

"The walk will be good for us," Juliana replied. "We've been sitting and driving so much we'll turn into fat gummy bears."

"The trail is three miles in, half of it uphill, then three miles back out. We can't camp out because we only have one sleeping bag. As interesting as that may sound, it doesn't work at all. So, we hike, dig, hike. We have about seven hours."

"Sounds like the Alcatraz Triathlon: Dig, Swim, Run," Juliana said.

"With about the same amount of time. Let's go."

The walk in was as beautiful as Austin remembered, only with many shades of green leaves now instead of orange, yellow, and red. They covered the level mile and a half quickly, the uphill mile and a half less so, and as they approached the pile of rocks Austin was looking for they saw a tent pitched nearby.

"Company," said Juliana, "Suppose anyone's home?"

They climbed the final distance and approached the tent. No one responded when Austin called out so he checked inside. Nobody there, but neatly arranged gear indicated someone had camped there or intended to.

"Probably out hiking," Austin said. "It's three in the afternoon; whoever it is will probably be back in the next couple hours."

"So, here we are at the digging part," Juliana said. "We should get it done right away before we have to explain what we're doing to someone."

She moved the rocks aside and began. Austin took over when she slowed down and in a little more than half an hour, Parcel Six was aboard. They filled the hole, replaced the rocks and smoothed out the area, then stood at the summit for a time just looking around at what Austin called the "quietude."

"Here comes the hiker," Juliana said. In the distance, they saw a woman walking toward them, her ponytail swaying back and forth.

"You again," she said upon arrival. "Didn't I see you here once before? From Kansas, wasn't it?"

"I was here before, in the fall," Austin replied, "except I'm from Oklahoma. A lot of people think I look like someone they know." He knew perfectly well it was the same person he'd met ten years before but wasn't going to say so.

"Well, you do look like one of my long-ago boyfriends," she went on. "Maybe it was you, maybe not. Anyway, I'm here because a hiker died on this trail last winter and some of his belongings were never retrieved. I thought I'd spend a couple of days looking to see what I could find."

"Any luck?" Juliana asked.

"Yeah, as near as I can tell he got way off the trail and fell on some rocks and hit his head. When he woke up, he crawled some distance but passed out again and eventually froze to death. He laid there several days before Search and Rescue found him. I located where it happened and found his canteen and flashlight some distance away."

"Two things he would have needed," Austin said.

"Yeah, it was too bad. The man wasn't experienced. He made a few mistakes and got lost."

"Things can go wrong in a hurry out here," Austin said.

"So true."

"We should go," Juliana said, "so we don't get lost in the dark."

"Good hiking," the woman said.

"Friend of yours?" Juliana asked as they made their way down the trail.

"I met her when I was here last time."

"But you didn't say so when she asked."

"No, it would have made things way too coincidental, especially when so much time has passed. We'd probably still be talking."

They were back in the car at seven o'clock.

"Only one more parcel to go," he said, "then we head home. I must say I've enjoyed having such pleasant company on this trip. I almost always drive alone."

"I've enjoyed it also but we don't have to burn up the roads going directly home," Juliana responded. "David and Rory have an extra parcel to retrieve, and we're coming up on the weekend, so we could easily make the trip last another two or three days. There's a lot of country to see and expense money to spend."

"Works for me," Austin replied. "We have mountainous driving between here and our next destination. You want to drive some of it off yet today?"

"No, I don't want to go any farther. I want something substantial and wonderful to eat and a margarita or two. We can be road warriors again tomorrow. And I want to go to Park City, Utah, on the way home."

"What's there?"

"The headquarters of Mrs. Field's Chocolate Chippery. Debbi Fields opened her business selling cookies from a cart in Palo Alto, California, then moved to Park City. As you said, it's one of those happened-to-be-in-the-neighborhood things."

"Sounds like a winner," Austin said.

CHAPTER 29

It Was Somewhere Around Barstow

Austin and Juliana ate breakfast early at the hotel, then headed west into Oregon on a route leading through mountains on twisting, turning roads, south through a more level landscape toward the Nevada border, then west again through an even more mountainous region to Klamath Falls and beyond.

"Sorry if I was cranky yesterday," Juliana said. "The hike was beautiful, but the day was getting pretty intense."

"Margaritas were a great alternative to pressing madly on," Austin replied.

"So, today's a bit of a grind?"

"Not difficult, just a lot of mountain roads. We're driving about 500 miles to Crater Lake, then into the National Park to where I buried Parcel One. Unfortunately, the place closes at five o'clock in June so we won't get there in time today. We'll have to wait until 9:30 tomorrow morning when they open."

"No rush, then."

"Nope, we can just be tourists enjoying the scenery and The Road today."

"But if we'd gone farther yesterday," Juliana observed, "we could have gotten to the park today before it closed."

"True story," said Austin.

"Okay, I get it. You weren't just being Mad Max."

"Not entirely, but there's no prize for getting done early. We're good where we are."

"A couple of times now," Juliana said, "you've said 'the road' as if it was some ceremonial or spiritual experience. Do I hear you wrong, or does it have a special significance to you?"

"The Road has answers," Austin replied.

"Answers to what?"

"I think of something I need resolved and sort of set it loose in my head. Driving gives it time to float around and bang into things and sometimes pick up pieces of a solution. When enough pieces come together, I can see the way to an answer."

"Sounds mystical," Juliana said.

"Not really. It's just a way of thinking about something without really thinking about it. Turn it loose and let it churn around; sometimes it solves itself."

"Give me an example."

"It was how I planned much of my original journey to hide parcels. I didn't sit down at a desk at the beginning and work it out. The most efficient way to do things gradually occurred to me as I drove."

"Awesome, I guess. I'll have to try it out. We have plenty of The Road left to do."

It wasn't a leisurely day for David and Rory. They took the Jersey Turnpike north past Philadelphia through New Jersey and into New York, then in totally bonkers traffic through New York City and the Bronx. They finally escaped into upper New York State, pushed on to Poughkeepsie where they stopped for pizza, then to Albany and east across the border into Vermont. Their destination was the Appalachian Trail crossing just outside Bennington. They found it on Vermont Highway 9 and parked the car in a pullout area.

"Your map notes say Parcel Five is buried behind a trail shelter about a mile and a half north of here," David said. "It's now mid-afternoon. Do you think you can get there and back before dark? I don't see much benefit in both of us going. I would just slow you down."

"Not a problem," Rory replied as he put the shovel in his pack. "It looks like easy going. I should be back by seven."

The route had only a thousand feet of elevation gain so he covered the distance in a little over an hour. He arrived to find three hikers in the shelter.

"Afternoon," he said. "Which way are you guys headed?"

"North," one replied. "We just stopped for another lunch. We'll go on to do more miles, maybe another eight or so, to the next shelter."

"Are you going north too?" another asked.

"No, I'm not hiking the AT," Rory replied. "A buddy of mine buried a food cache somewhere around here but never used it. He got injured and had to leave the trail. He asked me to come to find it for him."

"How long ago did he leave the trail?" asked the third.

"It was sometime last year."

"Geez, do you think the stuff is still any good?"

"Sure, backpacking food lasts forever, doesn't it?" said Rory.

"Usually, and if it goes bad, we hardly notice."

"What was your buddy's trail name?"

Rory's knowledge of Appalachian Trail lore was limited and the conversation was heading perilously into unknown areas. He needed to end the chatter quickly before he made some obvious misstep.

"I think it was Rutabaga, or Rubber Duck, or something similar. I only heard him mention it once. Anyway, I need to find this and get back to the car before dark. You guys have a good hike."

"Need any help?"

"No, I'm good, thanks," Rory said.

He activated the beacon with his phone and quickly located the spot to dig. He wandered back and forth a bit, making a show of searching for markers, then started digging. He was about two feet down when the other hikers donned their packs and hit the trail.

"Find it?" one asked as they were leaving.

"I think so," said Rory, and he waved them goodbye.

He pulled the plastic tub out a short while later and secured it in his pack. He filled the hole, and since it was now all downhill, leisurely headed back the way he'd come. He reached the car with plenty of daylight remaining and immediately boxed up Parcel Five for mailing.

"Good going, Rory," David said. "I found some great places to eat between here and Bar Harbor while you were gone."

They had one parcel yet to find, about seven hours away in Maine.

Sandra drove west after their night in Flagstaff, following I-40 through land empty of much civilization and into an even more empty stretch in California. The road seemed to go endlessly on and on and never change, offering only an occasional sign telling them they weren't getting much of anywhere. It was somewhere around Barstow the remote and distant emptiness of the land began to take hold.

"Lord, this is tedious," Caroline said when it was her turn to drive. "Nothing but desert wherever you look. I haven't seen anywhere to eat or drink or get gas in hours."

"The sun is shining," Sandra replied cheerily, "and we're almost to Barstow."

"The sun is always shining in Barstow."

"I'm sure there'll be something to eat there, and we'll switch to I-15

141

going south. Then we go through Oceanside and on to Escondido where we'll find Parcel Eight."

"I'm getting to be glad this is our final stop," Caroline added. "We'll still have a couple thousand miles to go but it'll be good to be going home."

Elfin Forest Recreational Preserve is a relatively small natural area located off I-15 in the mountains west of Escondido, California. They drove through the city, then along twisting and climbing mountain roads to the park entrance and parked in the area provided. The preserve featured 11 miles of hiking trails, lovely mountain views, and abundant blooming flowers of the season. But the two tired travelers were way beyond scenic vistas and pretty flowers. They had one thing in mind: following the red dot to the place to dig.

It was late and the park was busy with Friday afternoon hikers. They'd driven eight hours of mainly boring desert to get here and weren't keen on waiting till every last visitor had gone home. The phone showed the parcel to be about a quarter-mile distant in what appeared to be a thick grove of trees.

"Let's give it a try," Caroline said, "and please, Universe, if you would be so kind, no snoopy hikers or park rangers wondering what we're doing."

"Or nosy old ladies with yappy dogs," Sandra added.

They increased their pace from its usual mosey to a double-mosey, left the trail at an appropriate spot and entered bordering trees, and soon were in dense woods with the dot now holding steady. No one could see them and they proceeded without interruption. They dug three feet down, collected the tub, filled the hole and smoothed it down, and were soon on their way back to the car.

"That's the end of it," Sandra said as she readied Parcel Eight for mailing. "Let's go to town. I'm thinking seafood for dinner; how about you?"

"Sure, and plenty of wine; I don't mind what color," Caroline replied.

CHAPTER 30

You Have No Jurisdiction Here

The law firm representing individuals suing the Xander Moorhouse Estate wasn't satisfied with No for an answer.

C. Monica had expected they wouldn't be. Saying No with dramatic formality had just been her opening move from the array of delaying tactics she could employ.

Having had no success obtaining Estate financial statements, the firm now asked for three years' tax returns, which was precisely the dance move C. Monica had anticipated. She'd never seen tax returns for either the Estate or Xander Moorhouse himself, but as appointed representative, she was authorized to request them for particular years from the IRS.

During his lifetime, tax reporting for Xander Moorhouse had been labyrinthine in complexity. The completed return often exceeded 500 pages listing rent and royalty income from dozens of properties, interest and dividend income from many bank and institutional accounts, miscellaneous revenue from other buy and sell transactions, plus excruciating details for the mountain of expense invoices from day-to-day property operation. Mowing grass, plowing occasional snow, repairing roof leaks and parking lots, replacing broken windows and air conditioning units – all done by contracted services which sent bills for categorizing, summarizing, reporting, and paying.

The process was much simpler now. Xander Moorhouse's tax return listed three foreign investment firms as sources of income, the amount received from each, and the resulting total tax due. True, the return did show names of the offshore investment firms and their location, but in blanks requesting "Account number or other designation," he'd entered Account Caroline, Account David, and Account Juliana.

The document still approached 100 pages by the time individual buy and sell dealings were reported, but its summary was still relatively simple: I took in this much, tax due is this much, here's my check.

Knowing the names of the foreign investment firms might seem at first a massive breakthrough for those who'd filed the suit but such knowledge would lead them nowhere. They'd need correct account numbers and passwords. Account Caroline, Account David, and Account Juliana wouldn't do the trick.

The Singapore investment firms would politely refuse all requests for information without complete and proper account identification. Whoever tried to insist in a diplomatic or intimidating manner they be given access, the answer would still be the same: you have no jurisdiction here, no access without identification.

C. Monica prepared forms authorizing sending requested tax returns to comply with the letter. The opposing law firm would now wait a month or more for returns to arrive, then spend another month in futile pursuit of banking information, and afterward devote time to coming up with their next new tactic.

It was just a way of running up the tab before eventually and inevitably advising their clients to give it up. At $500 per hour, or perhaps even $750, they could bill $100,000 for just writing letters now and then and looking busy.

There was no forecast of how long this would continue. Move, countermove ... move, countermove ... the contest would go on until someone ran out of money. It might get ugly or simply drift along as lawyers piled up hours and sent monthly itemized bills.

C. Monica could employ ugly tactics, too. It wasn't her preferred way of doing things but she was by no means unprepared. She hadn't become administrator of her own prestigious law firm by being all smiley and nice.

As a precaution, and to resolve a nagging suspicion, she called all-purpose firm researcher Sydney to her office.

"I have a project for you," she said. "Xander Moorhouse, one of our clients, sold about 25 pieces of property over the past 15 or so years."

"I'm familiar with him," Sydney said. "I think I worked on his file."

"I want you to find out who purchased each property, get their backgrounds, and see if any common threads run through them. Three of those purchasers are suing the Moorhouse Estate. What I want to know is how these three are connected, if they are, and whether there are any other such connections we should be concerned about."

144

"So, maybe others are waiting to see how this suit goes so they can file one of their own."

"Exactly," C. Monica said.

It was Tuesday morning. Late Thursday afternoon Sydney had several pages of beautifully handwritten notes together with a few lines of conclusions.

"Purchasers are from all over the South but nine are in Oklahoma," she reported. "The three presently suing Moorhouse live here in Oklahoma City, four others are in Tulsa, and two are in Bartlesville. The rest are in Kansas, Texas, Arkansas, and Georgia.

"Those here in town belong to the Lions Club and likely go to a nearby bar after meetings. Three of the four in Tulsa race stock cars, and there's no apparent connection to the two in Bartlesville. One of those here in town also has a car he runs at Tulsa Raceway Park.

"There may be a connection among the stock car enthusiasts. I can dig deeper if you'd like."

"Excellent work," C. Monica said. "Narrow focus to those individuals to see if you find anything there."

Sydney was back the next day after using her considerable account hacking skills to probe beyond the obvious.

"Purchasers who filed the suit are in financial trouble," she said. "They overextended their capacity for new investment when they bought the Moorhouse properties and now are having trouble finding tenants for newly acquired space. Their cash flow will dry up if things don't improve for them soon. The same is true of two purchasers in Tulsa."

The take-away was three purchasers were suing to recover from their bad judgment and a similar suit might follow.

"Thank you so much," C. Monica said. "I'm not sure what to do with this information but it's what I vaguely suspected. So, I'll take it from here."

"By the way," she said as Sydney got up to go, "I understand you're leaving us."

"I am," was Sydney's reply. "I'm moving to North Dakota, probably in late July. The recent oil boom there is fading now but companies have an urgent need for programmers to clean up messes left from several years of frantic activity."

"They have winter there," C. Monica said.

"Indeed they do, and bleak, windswept prairies. I'll take refuge behind my keyboard and try not to overthink it."

145

"May I ask why you're moving on?"

"It's the lure of something new, I suppose," Sydney answered. "Everything here is running smoothly and there's not much more I can see to do. The new job will likely be a total disaster where programmers with questionable abilities have thrashed and blundered about making things worse. The challenge of cleaning it up is what's attractive. I have the skills. I'm curious to see if I can put them to work effectively in the oilfields."

"Well, best of luck; we'll miss you. You've done nearly ten years of fine work for us."

"Thank you," Sydney said as she departed, "It's been a great ten years. I'll miss everyone here as well."

Meanwhile, Becky had reported the family adventurers' successful retrieval of 15 parcels to date. Caroline and Sandra were headed back to Oklahoma City; Juliana and Austin were poised to get their final parcel as soon as Crater Lake Park opened for the day. David and Rory were on their way to Maine.

It was Friday, which meant they'd all be back in town by the middle of next week. They'd be eager to open parcels and see what their father's elaborate plan was all about, if there actually was one. More to the point, they'd want details on his legendary fortune and whether he'd left some part of it to them.

With all this soon to be in place, it was finally time for C. Monica to set the stage for the drama's last act.

CHAPTER 31

Is It Too Early for a Margarita?

Juliana drove into Crater Lake National Park a few minutes after it opened. She took the West Rim Road and followed it until Map Lady announced they were nearing their destination. The sky was dark with clouds and a gentle misty rain was just beginning. Not the least bothered, they slipped into the woods guided by blinking and beeping from Austin's phone, dug and retrieved Parcel One, and returned to the car.

Juliana was boxing it up for mailing when a Park Ranger truck pulled up and stopped next to them.

"Good morning, sir," Austin said in his best respectful tone.

"Good day to you folks as well," the Ranger replied. "I'm looking for a lost hiker. I wondered if you'd seen anyone on the road."

"No, we haven't," Juliana said. "How long has this person been missing?"

"He – Roger is his name – started hiking the 33-mile trail around the lake a few days ago. He supposedly planned to finish in one day but didn't show up at his meeting place. He's not well-equipped and could be in trouble."

"A pretty long haul for one day," Austin said.

"It is, and some of these kids overestimate their endurance and run out of gas halfway round. We have a few people out looking; I saw you parked and thought I'd ask."

The Ranger glanced into the back of Austin's car and couldn't help noticing the mailing box Juliana was working on, the protective bag she'd removed from the parcel, and, most conspicuous of all, the unfolded camp shovel.

"We were looking for a spot to bury a food box for resupply," Austin said by way of explanation, "but this one didn't turn out very well. We'll have to keep looking."

"Burying food is a good backpacking strategy," the Ranger replied, "but remember, you need a backcountry permit for your hike. You can get them by mail or at the Visitor Center."

"We'll do so when we figure out where we're going," Juliana said.

"You also should be careful to bury it deep enough and in some kind of container to keep animals from smelling whatever you're burying."

"We're using these," Austin showed him the odor-proof bag removed from Parcel One. "We can fold them up and use them again or burn them in the campfire."

"This one seems to have served you well," the Ranger commented.

"Yeah, and it still works."

"Okay, then, have a pleasant day. If you see lost Roger anywhere, please give him a ride." The Ranger got in his truck and drove off.

"Lost Roger," Juliana said. "If we found him, would he be Jolly Roger?"

"Probably."

"If we asked him to do something, would he say 'Roger that'?"

Austin didn't reply as Juliana resumed the drive around Rim Road.

"Meanwhile, ta-da, just to make it official: we're done," she went on. "We've dug up and claimed all the parcels you spent 18 months squirreling away."

"Exactly so," Austin said. "David and Rory will collect their last one today."

"Do we celebrate something, or anything? It's Friday; we could celebrate Friday."

"I'm thinking celebration depends on what's actually in the parcels."

"Oh, bother, what's in them is next week's problem," Juliana said. "Think about today. Is it too early for a margarita?"

"It's five o'clock in Greenland, I think."

"Good enough. Let's get lunch and get going. Since we're taking the long way home, how far will we be traveling?"

"About 1,900 miles through six or seven states," Austin said. "It's at least a three-day trip, plus time for things to see and do along the way."

"Like getting chocolate chip cookies in Park City."

"Wouldn't miss it for anything. Is there anywhere else you'd like to go?"

"I don't know," Juliana said, "but maybe if we listen to The Road it will tell us."

They didn't find Roger but discovered a Mexican restaurant for lunch and ordered Margarita Grandes and chips, refills of chips, and even more chips.

"So, what do you actually do to pass the time when you're driving these long distances?" Juliana asked. "You've been pretty quiet on this trip. Besides letting problems in search of solutions roll around in your head when you're alone, do you sing or recite poetry, listen to music or books, pick up hitchhikers, have conversations with Map Lady?"

"I watch what's going on outside. The windshield view changes, sometimes very quickly, from beautiful to boring to fascinating to occasionally even scary. Interstates can be unexpectedly scenic at times, majorly ho-hum sometimes, other times desolate. Stormy weather brings new conditions and each has its particular charm or complete lack of it.

"As for Map Lady, she's not much on conversation. Call her a nasty name and she gets upset, but otherwise she sticks to business. She has other voices, by the way. There's a British accent selection as well as a man's voice you can choose."

"If it's not James Earl Jones," said Juliana, "I'm not interested."

"Right, I can just hear his deep voice booming out, 'Turn left NOW.'"

"So, you're thinking having somebody along is a good thing?"

"Having you along has been good. You're enjoyable company."

"And we have three more days," she said with a smile.

David and Rory headed east through New Hampshire to Portsmouth and the turn north into Maine. They had about half a day's driving to get to Bar Harbor and entry to Acadia National Park.

"Becky says the others are heading home," David said.

"Too bad for them," Rory replied. "We have miles and miles of fishing villages and lobster. It's great you had so much expense money. This trip has been like a free vacation for me: lots to see, lots to eat, and all I had to do was a little driving."

David was silent for a time, then said: "One thing I'll say for your grandfather is he was certainly generous, in fact overly so. He gave the three of us each $10,000 for this trip. We won't even spend half of it. Not to go all Freudian here," he went on, "but I'm sure some would say his over-generosity was him compensating for years of not paying attention to his family."

"Whoa, deep," said Rory.

"I'm not stupid, you know, even if everyone thinks so."

"Then I say hats off to Mr. Moorhouse," Rory said. "Yay, Gramps."

They drove through Augusta and Bangor, then turned east toward Bar Harbor.

"Looks like we'll get there about five o'clock," Rory observed. "Let's get dinner, then head into the park afterward to get the parcel. Acadia is open 24 hours a day so we can go in late and get our work done with fewer people around."

"Excellent," said David. "So, lobster for dinner, is it? We had lobster for lunch."

"Is there a problem in there somewhere?" Rory said.

"Certainly not," David answered.

They ordered as much lobster as they could eat at the Bar Harbor Lobster Company and waited patiently, anticipating its superb, delicate taste.

"Would you like to try a Boulevardier?" David asked.

"Hmm ... a beer on the beach was great," Rory replied, sounding uncertain, "but aren't I a bit underage for ordering hard liquor in a restaurant?"

"I suppose so, but as your uncle, I can be considered your guardian, and it's fine with me."

"That works; so what's a Boulevardier? I've never tried many mixed drinks."

"It's made with rye whiskey, sweet vermouth, and Campari, a bitter red liqueur. It's mixed in more or less equal parts and garnished with an orange or cherry. I think it would be just the thing with lobster. It's not usually on a regular cocktail menu. Sometimes I have to tell the bartender how to make it."

"Okay, I'm in."

Rory took a tentative sip when it arrived, squinted his eyes just a little, then took another sip.

"I think I could get to like this," he said. "I feel my horizons expanding already."

"Accept no substitutes," David said. "Now, where's our lobster? It's been hours since we had any."

They drove into the park about seven o'clock and followed GPS coordinates to Schooner Head Overlook. After walking down to water's edge for the mandatory visit to Anemone Cave and its residents, they retraced their steps uphill to the spot the locator beacon showed on their phone map.

A few people were at the overlook reading information displayed there, but none paid them any attention. They dug up Parcel Nine, shared an enthusiastic high-five, and returned to the car. Rory put the parcel in its mailing box to send off at the next post office they passed.

"How far away is home, 2,000 miles?" David asked.

"Pretty close," Rory replied, "it'll take us into next week. But first, another Boule-whatever-it-is. It was excellent."

"Let's hear it for the corruption of youth," David said.

Part Three — Reckoning

CHAPTER 32

Whoever Found It Gets to Open It

Monday, July 9, began poorly for C. Monica Stansbury, Esq.

She was scheduled to meet with the Moorhouse heirs at two o'clock and she'd assigned a clerk to lay parcels out in sequence as the long-planned meeting format required. But the entire event suddenly plunged into dark uncertainty when the clerk nervously reported four words:

"Parcel Nine is missing."

C. Monica was silent as questions flooded her mind. Missing where? Missing how long? Missing from the building or just misplaced? Who had access to a locked closet in the conference room? How to find Parcel Nine without accusing 50+ high-priced lawyers and staff of petty thievery?

"Not good news," she said absently while her mind raced on. After more silence, during which her expression descended fully into grave concern, she did what everyone else in the office did when they had a problem.

"Find Sydney," she said to the anxious clerk. "I want to see her right now."

Sydney appeared a few minutes later.

"Something vital is missing," C. Monica said. "I need your help to find it." She explained the afternoon arrival of the Moorhouse children and the missing parcel.

"Are you certain you ever had it?" Sydney asked.

"Yes, I kept them locked in the conference room closet and all 17 were there yesterday."

"How did you discover one missing?"

"My clerk was unboxing and preparing them for the meeting. She noticed it partway through the process."

"Is she still there?"

"Very likely," C. Monica said, "and I'm sure she's expecting me to shoot the messenger."

"Please, don't do that," Sydney said. "I'll take it from here."

Sydney found the clerk in the conference room, digging through trash, fussily arranging things for no apparent purpose, and on the verge of tears.

"I want to help you fix this," Sydney said. "Tell me what you've been doing."

"Ms. Stansbury unlocked the closet and showed me mailing boxes she'd stacked there. I was to open each one and remove packaging from what was inside until I got to the actual parcel. Then I'd stick a label on it telling who'd mailed it and from where and arrange them in numbered sequence. There are supposed to be 17 of them. I didn't count to start with, but it seemed there weren't that many. As you can see, they're all in place except Parcel Nine. I feel terrible about this. I hope I don't get fired."

"The time to feel terrible is when we can't find it," Sydney said encouragingly. "Show me the trash."

The clerk showed her a pile of discarded heavy black plastic bags, a stack of empty white tubs, the original Post Office mailing boxes, and a small container of what appeared to be electronic devices.

"What are these?" she asked the clerk.

"I don't know, but I found one in each of those white things along with the parcel itself."

Sydney inspected one and located a manufacturer's number of some kind. Moments later, she read about it on her phone: a locator beacon – how ingenious. She downloaded the application provided, activated it, and her phone instantly lit with 16 overlapping red dots on a map of the Stansbury building vicinity. She instructed the clerk to guard contents of the room at all costs, then walked through the entire building with the app turned on. Aside from the conference room, there were no red dots or beeps. She went next to the firm's receptionist.

"Can you tell me how many employees didn't report to work today," Sydney asked.

"Yes, I can," she replied cheerfully and began scrolling her computer screen. "Seven lawyers aren't here today," she replied after a minute or so, "four are out of town, and three are in court. Of the clerical and office staff, three aren't here, at least not so far."

"Please send me home addresses of the three in court and the three office staff," Sydney said.

"You'll have them right away," the receptionist replied. She hadn't asked why Sydney wanted this information or if she had authorization. No one asked Sydney such things.

Then Sydney began driving, first through the Stansbury parking lot, then the lot at the courthouse. There was no response at either. Next came individual addresses. A dot began to show as she neared the fourth on the list.

Sydney parked at the curb, approached the house, and knocked on the door. A slender man of recent college graduate age answered.

"Give me the package," Sydney said as greeting.

"Package?" the man said. "What package?"

"The one this phone says is here," and she held up the phone for him to see the blinking red dot and hear the sound of rapid beeps.

He appeared to be mustering bravado for further denials, but caved in Sydney's withering presence.

"It's on the kitchen table," he said. "You might as well come in."

Sydney walked directly to it. "Did you open it?" she asked.

"No, I didn't. I didn't know what to do with it. It was just a prank that seems to have become a terrible idea. I mean, it's not even noon and here you are, found me already."

"How did you find it, and what made you choose this one?"

"I kept hearing about the parcels around the office. I was there late last night and thought I'd check them out. I picked the lock into C. Monica's conference room, found the parcel stash and took one off the top. It was heavy so maybe I thought it was full of cash. Sheesh, this was just supposed to be a joke."

"Well, sir," Sydney said, "welcome to the real world. Pranks aren't a big thing in business offices, especially in a whole building full of lawyers. Whatever were you thinking?"

"I regretted it before I was even halfway home. I guess I should have turned around and put it back."

"I'm leaving now," Sydney said. "What you do next is up to you. But meanwhile, congratulations, you just lost your first job."

"I'm fired?"

"Not by me. You'll have to make your peace with C. Monica about that."

154

Sydney departed and immediately texted C. Monica: "I have Parcel Nine. On my way."

Caroline, David, and Juliana appeared promptly as scheduled.

"Thank you for coming," C. Monica began, "and thank you for diligent recovery of all 17 parcels. I've had them removed from their protective containers and verified all were intact and unopened. I'm pleased you followed your father's directions. This gathering would be truly awkward if you hadn't." She didn't mention the morning's tense drama but was visibly relieved to know the Seventeen Parcels were all in place.

"Today, we begin the long-awaited task of opening each parcel," she went on. "As I told you weeks ago, we'll do so in sequence: One through Seventeen, because your late father directed me to do it this way. In addition, and this is also his requirement, we'll open a specified number of them each day this week, finishing up with the final parcels on Friday.

"I do not know what's in them; only your father knew. But as he was and still is my client, I must proceed according to his wishes. These parcels are your legacy to use or interpret as you will. Do you have any questions?"

"You didn't invite Austin?" David said. "He was very helpful to us."

"No, this process is only for immediate family. Further involvement of Mr. Somerfeld will be at your choosing."

"Same for Sandra and Rory, I presume?" said Juliana.

"Correct. If you benefit, it's up to you to choose whether they do also. Now, if you have no further questions, please follow me to the conference room and we'll begin."

They walked down a short hallway to a room with the parcels set out in sequence on a long table. Once the three heirs were seated at a separate table, C. Monica brought Parcel One.

"This is now yours. Open it however you decide."

"How about this for an idea," David said: "whoever found it gets to open it."

"Do we even remember who found which one?" Caroline asked.

"Not a problem," David answered, "there's a sticker on this one telling us. I presume the rest have stickers as well. Juliana, the first is yours."

"Seems like we just dug this one up," Juliana observed. She broke the seal on the parcel and remove the lid. It contained only an envelope addressed to the three of them. She opened it.

"It's a letter from dad," she said.

"Read it to us, if you would, please," said David.

Juliana began.

My Dear Children:

I accumulated a fortune valued somewhere over one billion dollars in my lifetime.

Sadly, it's my only notable life accomplishment. I genuinely regret being so focused on getting rich instead of spending more time with you, learning more about you, and being helpful when you needed it. Only your mother was responsible enough to do that.

What I have for you here at the end of my life may be a poor substitute for an interested father, but it's what I have. These 17 parcels are organized to help you understand more about me and help you deal with what I've left behind.

(Signed) Xander Moorhouse

Juliana put the letter down. There were gasps and looks of astonishment around the table.

David looked dazed. "A ... billion ... dollars," he was muttering.

"That's it?" Caroline said heatedly. "Just those few words?"

"He signed it," Juliana replied, "otherwise yes, it's all he wrote."

"So, in other words, dad says hello," Caroline said. "Hello from 10 or 11 years ago; not a big help."

"We should probably remember circumstances changed since then," said Juliana.

"I suppose," Caroline said, but she was clearly upset.

"A ... billion ... dollars," David was still saying.

"You okay there?" Caroline asked him.

"What?" he replied after a moment. "Oh, yeah, I'm okay."

"Well, we now know one thing for sure," said Juliana, "dad did have a fortune. So, let's move along and maybe learn more about it."

C. Monica handed them Parcel Two. Still a bit dazed, David opened it to reveal a box full of earrings, necklaces, bracelets, and the like.

"It's mom's jewelry," Caroline said, "at least some of it."

"Some of her good stuff is here, but not all," said Juliana. "She had many more lovely expensive things."

156

"Maybe the rest is stored somewhere else," David said. "Meanwhile, you two can divide this up however you like. You don't want to sell it, do you?"

"We'd never sell mom's stuff," Caroline answered, "would we, Juliana?"

"No, but maybe Sandra or Becky would like to wear some of it."

"There are many lovely things here," said David. "If you ever get invited to a fancy ball at Cinderella's castle, you're all set. Just remember to take me along as chaperone."

"We'll keep you in mind," Caroline said. "Now, on to the next, it appears."

C. Monica brought them Parcel Three and Caroline took charge. She slit the seal, removed the lid, and revealed a box full of bundles of hundred-dollar bills.

"Wow," David said, "this just got a whole lot more interesting."

"Bands around the bundles say each one is $10,000," Caroline replied, "and there are (she counted) 15 of them. Pretty easy to divide up," and she distributed bundles around the table like a Blackjack dealer until they each had $50,000.

"So, a box full of actual cash has been buried in the dirt in a campground in Nebraska for 11 years," Juliana said, "and here it is safely delivered to us.

"It rained there, it snowed, it may have frozen, and people walked overtop it. No one found it. No one stole it. It's not a redeemable certificate – it's real, spendable cash aged 11 years in dirt. Dad sure had a lot of confidence in this process he thought up."

"I'm sure Austin's thorough packaging made a big difference," Caroline said.

"And what a great beginning," David added. "Dad certainly has my attention, as if the billion dollars news didn't get it. I'm going to chalk this up as a truly worthwhile afternoon."

"We're at the end of our work for today," C. Monica said. It was barely 3:00; the whole process had taken only an hour. "We'll continue tomorrow same time. Meanwhile, I urge each of you to take the cash directly to your bank and deposit it."

"Do we need an armed guard?" asked Caroline.

"I can give you deposit bags and have Building Security drive you if you wish."

"Yes, please do so," said David. "We wouldn't want to lose it."

CHAPTER 33

Moved Millions of Dollars Somewhere

"Welcome to Day 2," C. Monica said when the Moorhouse heirs were assembled the following afternoon. "We'll open the next four parcels today, but first, I should inform you that three individuals are suing the Moorhouse Estate for $250 million and there's the possibility of another suit to follow."

"What on earth for?" asked David.

"These individuals – buyers of some of your father's properties – have joined forces to take advantage of his death to recover part of their purchase price. They apparently figure you, the heirs, won't be familiar enough with the situation to make an effective defense. In other words: they think you're easy pickings."

"Very true, sad to say," David said. "We don't know a thing about what dad was doing."

"Nor do you need to. This law firm will continue to represent you. We've handled matters like this before and they follow a predictable path: after a long series of creative legal gyrations from both sides, suits and countersuits often lasting years, during which time no one makes any money but us lawyers, they lose.

"If it looks like something different might happen, I'll work out a course of action with you. But meanwhile, we do the work, the Estate pays the bills, and we recover the expense when we win at the end.

"But now it's our Estate paying those bills," Caroline said. "Shouldn't we be watchful of how much it's costing? Are you eating into our inheritance?"

"Possibly," said C. Monica, "but we don't know yet what your inheritance is, or if there's any at all beyond the cash you received yesterday."

"At least that's safe," Caroline said, "or will be once the bank gets through fiddling with it. Maybe we should have just put it in our sock

158

drawers."

"Let's continue, shall we?" C. Monica said. "Looks like you're ready for Parcel Four." She handed it to them.

"Rory and I found this in Greenville, North Carolina," David said.

"Where you were dodging police, right?" Juliana said.

"Yes, but it wasn't serious. Everyone was polite and we got our job done without problem. It was a bit dark and rainy, though. Let's see what we dug up."

David opened it revealing three hardbound copies of The Moorhouse Family.

"We have history?" he asked, handing copies to each of the other two. "I guess we can read about our ancestors."

"Yeah, all the way back to the Eleventh Century," said Caroline, paging through it.

"I never knew this book existed," Juliana said. "Do you suppose we're in it?"

"What have we done to merit mention?" David asked. "Not much is my guess. We might have to wait a hundred years for the next edition."

"Speak for yourself," Juliana replied. "There might be enough drama in remaining parcels for us to write the next edition."

"I'll take my copy home to read and see if I can stay awake," Caroline said.

"It's your turn again, David," C. Monica said.

David opened Parcel Five and found a collection of newspaper clippings. He flipped through them briefly, began laughing, then passed several to Caroline and Juliana.

"These are stories about How Winning the Lottery Ruined My Life," David said. "This one's about a guy who ended up with $45 million or so after taxes. He bought a big expensive house, many new cars, a yacht, an airplane, a couple of custom-built motorcycles, and a $750,000 wristwatch. The money ran out after a year but he still had to pay monthly upkeep. Next thing he knew, banks and dealers repossessed everything and he was flat broke again."

"Here's a guy who drove around with most of a million in cash in a cardboard box in the front seat of his car," said Juliana. "He ran up a big tab buying everyone drinks at a bar one night; came out and found the box of money gone. Here's the real You-Can't-Fix-Stupid part of it: he did the same thing again two weeks later."

Everyone, including C. Monica, shook their head and rolled their eyes.

"This one is about someone winning $200 million," Caroline chipped in. "Total strangers from all over suddenly came out of the woodwork, writing him pleading letters, calling him on the phone, showing up at his door claiming to be his best friend of long ago or his aging aunt or uncle. And they all somehow desperately needed money. Gee Willikers, Mr. Science, who would have ever guessed?"

"He paid college bills for everyone in the family, bought his mom a new house, gave money to everyone with a sad story and pretty soon his winnings were gone. From $200 million to gone in under six months."

"Here's a story about a lottery winner support group," David said. "Big winners who turn themselves into big losers get together and boo-hoo each other about how they'd ruined their life and they wish they'd never won. Like it's the money's fault they're so dumb. Dad's maybe being a bit obvious here, you think?"

"Leading the witness," said Juliana, "especially with the story I saw of someone who invested his umpty-ump millions of winnings in apartment buildings and rental properties, then lived off the income. Sounds like good money management, I suppose, but it makes a boring story."

"I could live with such a boring story," Caroline said. "What's next?"

C. Monica handed them Parcel Six and Juliana opened it.

"Well, here you are, David, just what you were wanting." She said and pushed the open box containing an impressive collection of men's expensive wristwatches, along with a dozen small fuzzy jewelry boxes containing cuff links and stick pins ranging from artfully severe to expensively gaudy.

"Outstanding," David said, "dear old dad just certified and outfitted me to chaperone you two to the fancy-dress Cinderella ball."

"Right," Juliana said with a laugh, "We'll have our driver pick you up."

It was again Juliana's turn. Parcel Seven contained bundles of account statements which she described to the others as she paged through them.

"It looks like these are dad's bank accounts … at least a dozen of them … and in all different US States. Wait a minute … wait just a minute … they all say Final Statement … and the balance on each one … is zero. These accounts are all closed. There's nothing here."

"Well," David said, "yesterday we got $150,000, today nets out to zero. Why do you think dad wanted us to see this? It sounds like his day-to-day business stuff to me. Close one bank account, open another. Not sure we're learning much here."

"Wait, there's more," Juliana continued. "Each account had a huge balance, like between a half-million and $3.5 million, which mysteriously went away just before the account closed."

"Define away," David said.

"I don't know, but he moved it all to some mysterious somewhere. It happened in every one of these accounts over several years."

"Okay, we'll put them in the Gone-but-not-Forgotten stack," said David. "What's next, or are we done for the day?"

"Yes, today's schedule is complete," C. Monica said. "You'll do the next three tomorrow."

"He moved millions of dollars somewhere," Caroline said. "Let's hope there's further explanation coming."

CHAPTER 34

I Didn't Know Dad Collected Things

They gathered in the Stansbury conference room for a third day of executing final wishes of their deceased father. C. Monica set Parcel Eight on the table, the one put in jeopardy when the university clock tower blew down in California.

"How is this going for you so far?" she asked.

"The cash was nice to get and easy to understand," Caroline replied, "and the jewelry. But the rest is starting to be a puzzle. Dad's working up to telling us something here, I'm pretty sure. If he put this in place 11 years ago, why didn't he just talk to us while he was still alive instead of going to all the expense and trouble of this treasure hunt? We were together a lot going over day-to-day work at The Board Room. It's not as though he was locked away in his office like before."

"Maybe once he had the project going, he thought he had to carry it out," David said.

"He might have had a change of heart at some point," Juliana added, "and Austin's work was too far along to shut down."

"Whatever the story, we have ten more chapters of it to go," Caroline said.

It was her turn, so she opened Parcel Eight.

"It's a book," she said, holding up a thick volume with a plain green hardbound cover, a gilt title on its spine.

"Not another family history book," said Juliana.

"No, it's Tender is the Night by F. Scott Fitzgerald."

"Anything special about it?"

"Well, it looks to be in excellent condition. There's no dust cover (Caroline flipped through the first few pages), but it appears to be a first edition published in 1934. Sounds kind of special, don't you think? It might be worth a ton of money."

"I didn't know dad collected things," said David.

"Neither did I," Caroline replied, "but from what we've been learning about him, I'm guessing dad wouldn't have just one book. This one is just a sample; there might be more somewhere."

"This is getting way more interesting," Juliana said. "Even after our trips to see the world with dad and being around him a lot over the last few years, we're finding out many things we didn't know and never guessed. It does make you wonder what's next. Which, I suppose, is the effect he was after."

"Every story has a beginning, a middle, and an end," David said. "We had a rousing beginning with bundles of cash, and now we're in the middle where we should be learning what the story is about. When we get to the end on Friday, it might not make much sense without the middle."

"Were those thoughts going somewhere?" Juliana said teasingly.

"I'm not exactly sure, now that you mention it," David said with a chuckle. "I meant we should pay attention. If dad is telling us something, we should try not to miss it."

David started on Parcel Nine.

"It's heavy but makes no sound at all when I shake it," he said. Removing the lid revealed a thick document filling the entire box.

"I think it's one of dad's tax returns," David said. "This whole box contains only one return; it's more than 500 pages long."

"I don't even begin to want to go through it," said Caroline, "but could you maybe find a bottom line somewhere? How much his income was and what taxes he paid? I'm sure it's why he left it for us to see."

David handed the box to C. Monica. "If you don't mind, please, what she said."

C. Monica paged quickly through the document looking for a specific set of pages.

"Here it is," she said after a time. "In this particular year, your father's business holdings earned $42,749,263. After offsetting expenses, he paid taxes of $7,328,519."

"Dad paid $7 million and change in taxes for one year?" Juliana said in astonishment. "So much for big breaks for the rich."

"A mind-boggling number," said David. "Do you suppose it was one of his good years or was it just so-so?"

"I'd sure call it a good year," said Caroline. "Making $35 million after taxes would certainly work for me."

"I'm sure it didn't happen by itself," Juliana said. "He must have done a lot of smart and strategic work for it."

"I guess our question still is: Where is it?" said Caroline.

C. Monica brought them Parcel Ten.

"It's light and jingly," Juliana said. Inside she found a ring of keys.

"Keys to what? There are six of them ... wait ... here's a list." She took an index card from the bottom of the box. "Bank names and addresses ... are these for safe deposit boxes, do you suppose?"

"If so, we should go open them," David said. "But none of us has authorization. How do we get authorized? Is showing up with a key good enough?"

"No, you need an original death certificate for each one," C. Monica answered, "plus your identification."

"Won't a death certificate copy do?"

"No, every transaction involving one usually requires an original certified copy. Go to the Department of Health to get those. They'll cost you $15 each."

"Hold on," said Juliana, "there are also phone numbers on the back of this card."

"Let me see the card if you would," David said. "I'll find out what they are." He got out his phone and punched in numbers, calling two of the three numbers on the card.

"Well, here's another puzzle," he said upon ending the conversations. "Both places I called have storage lockers for rent. Maybe dad has stuff stored there. I got their addresses and they're here in town."

"You should check those out now," Caroline said. "Juliana and I will get the certificates while the Health Department is still open."

"It'll be too late for the banks," Juliana said. "We'll divide them up and go for safe deposit boxes tomorrow morning."

"Good idea," David said, "but just make lists of what's in them; don't remove anything. Dad must have put things in safe storage for a reason."

"Are we finished opening parcels for today?" Juliana asked.

"Yes, we are," said C. Monica. "I'll see you all here tomorrow."

Caroline and Juliana headed immediately downtown. They arrived within half an hour of closing time and obtained the six certificates they would need.

David drove to the first storage place he'd called. It was still open and he identified himself to the man at the counter.

"I think my deceased father, Xander Moorhouse, may have things stored here," David said. "Do you possibly have a record of it?"

"I'm sure we do," the man said. "Let me check." He entered the

Moorhouse name in the computer and it immediately displayed a list.

"Here we are: your dad has 14 pieces of art stored here. Would you like to see them or remove them from storage?"

"No, but I'm wondering what they are."

"I have photos of them," the man said, turning the screen around, "take a look."

David scrolled through them. He saw no big-name artist works but there were pleasing watercolors of rocky coastlines, autumn mountain meadows, colorful boats in a harbor, along with a variety of action paintings – speeding cars, horseraces, racing sailboats, and the like – and a few showing activities on the Stock Exchange floor.

There was also a large formal portrait of their mother. She smiled pleasantly at him from the computer screen and looked just as he remembered.

"Thank you so much," he said to the counterman. "I may want to remove some of these but not today."

"Just let me know," the man said.

The process went the same at his second stop. He found a collection of 137 vinyl phonograph records from all eras and music styles: Muddy Waters, Kingston Trio, Miles Davis, Jack

Teagarden, Grateful Dead, Herb Alpert, Tommy Dorsey, just to name a few. Nothing was especially rare or valuable. It looked like a collection their father had gathered through his college days but didn't want to store in the attic.

The business was about to close, so he departed. He'd check out the third phone number in the morning.

165

CHAPTER 35

May Not Be All Sunshine and Bunnies

The safe deposit boxes were at six different banks.

Caroline and Juliana went to three each, gained access, then picked through box contents in private rooms provided. They were alternately mystified and surprised at what they found and made brief lists of contents as David had suggested.

David's third phone number led to yet another storage place. There he found a bin of baseball artifacts: a bat signed by Ted Williams; a dozen baseballs with signatures including Babe Ruth, Warren Spahn, Reggie Jackson, and the entire 1955 Brooklyn Dodgers team; a second baseman's glove autographed by Red Schoendienst; plus other items from supposedly famous individuals David had never heard of.

Dad was a big baseball fan, David thought. Who would have figured that?

The heirs met for lunch at a restaurant Juliana had recommended.

"Well, wasn't this a fun morning," said Caroline after she'd ordered.

"For sure," David replied. "What did you discover?"

"One box is full of books, first editions like the Fitzgerald," Caroline said. "Beatrix Potter, J.D. Salinger, Agatha Christie, A.A. Milne, and others, about 12 of them altogether, some signed by the author.

"The second has the rest of mom's jewelry, the good stuff, probably worth many thousands of dollars.

"The third box I opened has a cigar box full of baseball cards. I think some of them might be rare because I vaguely remember the names from when I grew up: Ty Cobb, Roger Maris, Pete Rose, Mickey Mantle, Joe Jackson, and lots of others."

"Baseball card value goes up and down," David said. "The market heats up when people are nuts about them and cools off when they're not. I found baseball items too at one of those storage places: a whole bin full of bats and balls and gloves signed by legendary players."

"What was at the other two?" asked Caroline.

"One has dad's vinyl record collection; the other is stacked full of art. I didn't see anything valuable but there's a great portrait of mom."

"Maybe we should hang it in The Board Room," said Juliana. "Then the whole family would be there."

"Great idea," David said. "What did you find?"

"The first box I opened has more books in it, first issue Ayn Rand and Harry Potter and Dr. Seuss and others.

"The second has small envelopes with stamps and coins in them. I'm guessing these are rarities of one kind or another but they're just in a pile, not in any order.

"The third is stuffed with comic books. I never read comics much as a kid so I didn't recognize any of them. But they're in protective envelopes and are first issues, or at least low issue numbers."

"Two things we've learned here," Juliana went on. "First, it looks like dad had a collecting habit, and second, he was serious about not putting all the eggs in one basket. He has stuff spread all over."

"I'm wondering if his collecting strategy was to pay top dollar for something interesting at auction," David said, "then just stash it away to let it get even more valuable. It wasn't in his nature to display things around the house so we never knew about any of it growing up."

"Having as much money as he did," Juliana said, "he didn't need to sell anything. Everything piled up more-or-less in a heap over the years and here we are finding the heap all at once."

"I think I understand now why he only wanted us to open a few parcels at a time," David said. "He's building his story bit by bit. Opening the parcels all in a day would spread those story bits all over. Some would overshadow others or get lost. This way, we're getting a chance to figure out where things fit."

"Well, to be a little less philosophical about it, we still have more to open," said Caroline. "Let's finish lunch and find out what else dad has in store?"

"You all look cheerful," C. Monica said when they arrived. "Was your trip to the bank successful?"

"Turns out Tender Is the Night first edition is just the beginning of dad's collection," David said. "He made lots of money and it looks like he spent a lot, too, on valuable things other than stocks and properties and land. We found more rare books, coins, stamps, baseball cards, a vinyl record collection, a bunch of old comic books, and a stash of art."

167

"Did your home have any of these items in it when you were growing up?"

"A lot of art on the walls," said Caroline, "but we grew up with it there and never paid it much attention. I don't remember anything valuable. Nothing dad fussed over and said not to touch, anyway."

"He apparently wasn't big on leaving clues scattered about," C. Monica said. "So, we have three more parcels to open today. We should get started," She handed them Parcel Eleven.

Caroline opened it to find a stack of paperclipped bundles of invoices and receipts.

"What's going on there?" Juliana asked.

"Let's see; it appears to be money dad spent on us. Here are cars he bought us … college bills he paid for those of us who went … money he gave some of us to start businesses … mortgages he paid off for us, and … oh, crap … who would save this kind of stuff … receipts for bailing David out of jail … geez, it looks like eight times."

"Awkward," David said.

"I guess he's telling us it's expensive to raise kids," Juliana said. "I don't remember him ever complaining about it, though. On the contrary, he always seemed okay with writing a check for something we needed or wanted."

"Until one day he wasn't," Caroline said. "At some point, he finally said we should make our own way. Things have been a lot tougher going since."

"Maybe that was his message," David observed.

C. Monica set Parcel Twelve on the table.

"We all found this one," Juliana said, "it was our test run to Muskogee, but it was Austin who made it possible."

"Why do I get the feeling you're kind of sweet on him?" Caroline asked.

"Probably because I am, a little. He's pleasant company. So, should I open this?"

"Go for it."

Documents jammed Parcel Twelve, bound together in three separate groups. She looked through opening pages of each bundle, shuffled quickly through the rest, then sat in silence with an odd look on her face.

"What do you have there?" David asked.

"I'm not entirely sure, but it appears to be movie and video rights to three different novels."

"Did anyone we've heard of write them?" wondered Caroline.

"I don't recognize the authors but the book titles seem vaguely familiar. What do you suppose we do with these?"

"I can help out there, if I may," said C. Monica. "If you want to make a movie from one or more of these novels, these documents give you the right to do so and the right to any money the movie earns. However, if someone else wants to make the movie, they must buy the rights defined in these documents from you at whatever price you negotiate."

"I suppose if nobody wants to make the movie, they're not worth anything," said Juliana.

"Very true," C. Monica said, "and they're surely not worth anything in a box buried in the ground. But you can hire an agent to shop them around, as they say in the trade. An agent could find or possibly develop interest."

"These novels were published 10 or 15 years ago," David said. "They may have racked up some sort of track record since then. We could check each book's sales history to see if it's enough to get someone interested."

C. Monica handed them Parcel Thirteen, the one Rory and David dug up in two feet of muddy water at the lake in Texas. David opened it to reveal another pile of documents.

"More account statements," he said and paused to look through them, "this time from brokerage firms, and they're all zero as well. Again, significant money balances build up over time, and then the entire amount goes to some mysterious somewhere at the end. Away. Didn't we say once before the money just went Away? I wonder where Away really is."

"Stay tuned," said Caroline.

"The plot is thickening," Juliana observed, "or dissolving, or vanishing, or bubbling, or something. I'm almost afraid to open the next one."

C. Monica intervened at this point.

"I think we've finished for today. Be back here tomorrow afternoon and open the final four parcels. Then you'll have the whole story your father had to tell."

"Somehow, I get the feeling tomorrow's when the hammer or the guillotine or the other shoe drops," David said, "and the result may not be all sunshine and bunnies."

CHAPTER 36

A Real Pearl-Clutching Moment

They'd gathered for the final time with C. Monica.

David looked puzzled. "So far," he said, "we've found $150,000 in one parcel, collections of jewelry in others, safe deposit box keys in another, and bunches of documents and account statements in others showing his money all going some mysterious somewhere. Dad is building a story of some kind here, I know, but it still seems random. Is there a pattern yet, something I should be seeing, or am I getting ahead of things, or behind things, or just a couple sandwiches short of a picnic?"

"There is a pattern," replied Juliana, "I think this whole elaborate discovery process we're in is slowly shaping itself into a big blinking pointer."

"Pointing to where the money went, you're thinking," David said.

"Exactly, it's pointing to Away. So, I think today's the day we find out where Away is."

"I hope so. There are four more chances. We'll soon see if you're right."

"Then let's get started," said Caroline. "I believe Parcel Fourteen is next."

She opened it to find a wad of e-mails and receipts and statements all paperclipped together.

"Boy, here's a puzzle." She paged slowly through documents and scraps of paper, pausing at some, flipping back to others, then going through them a couple of times again.

"Just a guess ... but it looks like dad kept large amounts of actual cash in several private vaults around the country. He hired armored cars ... they hauled it to local banks ... the banks did something with it and charged him a bunch of money ... and eventually they credited what was left back to him.

"He then put the money in his magic somewhere, and wherever said somewhere is, this bundle of transactions adds up to another $41 million going to it."

"Sounds like Away is adding up, heading toward the billion dollars dad mentioned," Juliana said. "Do you think we'll find Smaug there, or Bruce Wayne, or Scrooge McDuck?"

David opened Parcel Fifteen. "Looks like a bunch of legal documents," he said. "Ms. Stansbury, maybe you can help me with this."

She thumbed slowly through the relatively large stack of stapled and paperclipped bundles, pondering each individually a short while, then moving on.

"These are Quitclaim Deeds," she finally said, "what's left from, let's see, about 25 of your father's real estate properties. These are closing documents prepared when he sold them; they specify the new owners, sale amounts, and terms."

"So, those are properties he once owned but doesn't anymore," David said. "If he sold them, the money went to some account and we already know accounts are all zero. Twenty-five properties," David mused, "which must be all of them. It sounds like he unloaded everything."

"And the proceeds all went Away," added Caroline. "Aha, there is a pattern here, said Captain Obvious."

"We need some background music," Juliana said. "Tension is building to a real pearl-clutching moment. Who's next?"

"You are," C. Monica replied, and she handed her Parcel Sixteen. Juliana stared at it a moment, then removed the lid. The parcel contained three thick account statements and a single envelope, which she opened.

"It's a list of names and phone numbers for KGI Securities, Citibank, and Maybank Kim, whoever they are."

"Give me a minute," David said and he started searching for those names on his phone. "KGI Securities is a brokerage firm in Singapore," he said, reading what he'd discovered. He looked up the others as well. "Citibank has an office in Singapore, and the Maybank one is there too.

"Do you suppose it's where dad's money went?

"Is Singapore Away?"

Juliana shuffled through the account statements.

"These are statements from those three firms," she said. "They show pages and pages of transactions dating over the last 15 years or so. At the end of each, the balance is certainly not zero.

"So, David, you're right, Singapore is the shadowy, mysterious Away we were looking for. Here is all of dad's money." Juliana began to laugh.

"What's funny?" David asked.

"What's almost hilarious is that this box, Parcel Sixteen, sat out in the open desert for coyotes to chew on and drag around for maybe years. The sun beat down on it day after day and month after month, now and then it got rained on, the wind howled around it occasionally and blasted it with blowing sand, yet here it is, the answer to everything, surviving its desert ordeal and now safely in our hands.

"We found the answer to dad's puzzle on a pile of rocks in the empty Nevada desert. I'm sure Austin never intended any of that to happen when he buried it, but what came close to being a disaster turned out a minor miracle."

"Not exactly funny, I'd say," David offered; "more of an Oh-My-God thing."

"If we have a list of bank or broker's names and phone numbers," said Caroline, "can we call them and get current account balances and have monthly statements sent to us?"

"I'm afraid such an approach won't work," said C. Monica. "You need a 21-digit account number for each and probably also a password and answers to security questions. I'm sure no such information is on the statements; they probably just show the last few digits of the account number, which isn't at all helpful."

"We can't just show up with these account statements and a death certificate?" asked Juliana.

"No, offshore banking laws are stringent and protective of the account holder. It doesn't matter who you are – another bank, the IRS, a creditor – even the account holder's heirs such as yourselves cannot gain access to any information."

"Then why did he give us phone numbers if they won't talk to us?"

"Oh, they'll talk to you, and you should go there," C. Monica replied. "I can prepare you proper introductions. You should meet your brokers and find out what exactly you can and can't do and what they'll do for you. I'm sure you'll be able to gain access to the accounts once you've established your credentials."

"Whoa," David said, "we'll have credentials. Don't we sound important!"

"Road trip!" Juliana said. "I'm up for it, but first, we need to hear the other shoe drop from Parcel Seventeen. Maybe it will change everything, or at least explain it."

172

CHAPTER 37

These Are Dad's Very Last Words

C. Monica brought them the final parcel. "You found this in Arizona," she said, "accompanied by unexpected drama, I understand."

"A flying pig, a shredded tire, directions taking us the wrong way, and 23 scruffy bikers who turned out to be perfect gentlemen," Caroline said. "It was certainly a dramatic afternoon."

She opened Parcel Seventeen. Like Parcel One four days before, it contained but a single envelope.

"Another letter from dad," she said, "his goodbye letter, I'm guessing."

"And so – drum roll, please – here we are at the end of things," David said. "We've done everything dad asked of us. We found out what his fortune is – a billion dollars – and we found where it is – 10,000 miles away and inaccessible to everyone, including us. Will this be a time for joy or sorrow, party hats or hankies? Please read it to us, big sister dear. We all await the answer."

"These are dad's very last words to us," Caroline replied. "I'd rather hear it than be the one to read it. So, Ms. Stansbury, will you please read this out loud. I think it's only proper for dad's chosen executor to tell us this long story's end."

"Of course," C. Monica said and she read the following letter:

Dear Caroline, David, and Juliana:

As you've learned from previous parcels, I have dissolved my entire portfolio of assets and transferred proceeds to three investment firms in the far-away country of Singapore. I did this to protect my estate from prying opportunists, from bad decisions, and please forgive me for saying so, from your own inexperience.

My holdings have increased to more than one billion dollars in value and will likely grow with good management. I've placed the entire amount into what is now known as The Moorhouse Trust.

Said Trust is a legal entity unto itself administered by investment brokers I've selected. They decide what to buy and sell based on my stated preferences, market trends and conditions, and their knowledge and experience. Their entire mission is to increase the portfolio's value.

In addition to these income-earning activities, The Moorhouse Trust has a schedule of regular disbursements. These are:

First, it pays Brokers and Trust Administrators their professional fees, along with any Federal taxes due.

Second, it maintains a retainer of $1 million to pay Stansbury Law Firm fees and expenses for representing first me, now the Trust, and also you in times you should require it.

Third, it pays expenses of the home you grew up in until you dispose of it if you so choose.

Fourth, it makes substantial contributions to charitable organizations I've judged worthy of support.

Fifth, final, and most important, it will distribute an annual amount of $1,000,000 to each of the three of you. You don't have to pass tests or meet standards to receive this. You've done what I asked of you to get this far.

You are my beloved children.

This amount is yours each year.

But you are not inheriting the entire accumulated fortune to do with as you will.

You are inheriting this fixed annual payment.

I have provided you with investment account statements and broker contact numbers to become familiar with the process and the investments themselves. You are welcome to contact these institutions and individuals to learn, as my heirs, what you may and may not do. But with or without your involvement, The Moorhouse Trust will continue to live on as an independent money-making engine.

Be aware there is no bail-out provision if you spend your money foolishly. Once your annual payment is gone, it's gone. There's no more until the following year. I'm sure you saw examples of unfortunate choices in the lottery-winner stories I provided. I encourage you to use your money wisely.

I've made no special provisions for your children, Caroline, your disabled wife, David, or your businesses, Juliana. These are personal issues for which I do not presume to reward or penalize. You've done a credible job of managing these matters and I'm sure you'll continue.

For your information, this is not the first version of this letter.

My original letter, written many years ago, was far less friendly as I'd believed you to be a great disappointment.

But these past many years of working with you day-to-day have been a great joy to me. You've shown a willingness to work and achieve and succeed on your own and have become children of whom I can be proud.

Thank you for giving me such a wonderful gift in my final years.

Farewell, my children. I'm glad I got to know you better.

(Signed) Xander Moorhouse

"Well ..." David said hesitantly, "now we know the whole story. I'm not entirely sure what to say."

"Dad didn't trust us with his money," said Caroline. "I guess I would have hoped he'd have more faith in us. On the other hand, he spent his life building this fortune and it was his to do with as he pleased."

"Looking at it practically," Juliana said, "what exactly would we *do* if he'd just given us the billion dollars? Divide it into thirds and go our own way with it? None of us has that level of money management skill. At least one of us would be broke in the first year."

"If we were smart – and there's no guarantee of that – we'd find someone to manage it for us," David said. "Well, guess what, dad did that for us."

"Having our family business at The Board Room has taken the pressure off," Caroline said. "We work at jobs and have our own income and I'm not desperate for cash like before. Dad slowly came to appreciate us for making the business happen. We would never have done it independently but it seemed to work once he got us going. I have to say it's probably best it turned out this way. Of course, the $1 million a year will be helpful as well. Rory and Sandra certainly have a more secure future."

"It's still enough money to start making dumb decisions," Juliana said. "Let's keep working as we're doing and not get tangled up with being rich."

"Works for me," David said.

"Me, too," agreed Caroline. "By the way, when does it start?"

"The first of next month," C. Monica replied. "And, as a bonus, even though more than half the year is gone, you still receive this year's full amount. Put it down to your father's uncommon generosity."

"I have to say," David began, "just reading dad's final letter to us without all the background drama of the 17 parcels wouldn't have been the same. All the run-up we went through gave us context and perspective. Now I understand what he did. I don't think I would have appreciated it otherwise."

"And so," C. Monica concluded, "this elaborate and highly engineered reading of Xander Moorhouse's will is now complete and I've explained all distribution terms. Do the three of you agree?"

"Yes," said David.

"I agree," said Juliana.

"I agree as well," Caroline said.

"Then, if you'll sign this closing document, you can go back to your lives and think about what you're going to do with them."

They each signed.

"Anyone up for going somewhere for a drink?" David asked.

"Thought you'd never ask," Caroline said.

"I'm in," said Juliana.

CHAPTER 38

Did They Tell a Story?

A letter from Stansbury Law Firm arrived in Austin Somerfeld's mailbox a month later.

The mailbox was attached to the same two-bedroom apartment at the same Oklahoma City address he'd had 11 years before.

Austin Somerfeld still lived there. He was still famous and still handled special driving requests from various sources.

The whole experience of going forth to hide a parcel somewhere every month was receding in his memory. He remembered occasional dramatic adventures and digging lots of holes, but each parcel was becoming just another of many thousands of deliveries he'd made over the years.

He remembered driving to retrieve parcels with Juliana. That week was still prominent in his mind because he'd never learned how it all turned out. What did they find when they opened them? Was it good or bad? Whatever the case, this too would eventually become just one more memory among many.

Which is why the letter from C. Monica took him by surprise.

The Seventeen Parcel Project was a success, she wrote, thanks in large part to him. According to original instructions from the client, Xander Moorhouse, she was hereby paying an additional bonus of $250,000. C. Monica thanked him for his careful and diligent work and wished him continued good health and fortune.

Austin was way beyond surprised: he was flat-out astonished. He'd received one bonus of $50,000; he never expected another, even larger one.

What to do, he wondered?

Send a thank-you letter?

Send an e-mail?

Go to her office to convey his appreciation in person?

For the moment, he sat in his old leather recliner and did nothing, letting his thoughts churn about until they pointed somewhere. When they did arrive at their destination, his face brightened with resolution.

He sent C. Monica flowers.

Even lawyers liked flowers.

Sydney Bridgewater did move to North Dakota. She did find work as a Computer Systems Analyst and did find new opportunities in the chaotic, free-wheeling oil fields to add substantially to her bank account. As before, she'd taken her time to get new code segments perfected and running, but now they were operational and paying off handsomely.

She'd achieved a career milestone of sorts before her move north: $10 million cash in the bank. The new code she'd just implemented would catapult her balance to possibly $13 million over just a few years. It was enough to move to an offshore account; she filed a mental note to book a trip to Switzerland.

Aside from such goings-on, specific ethical and procedural questions might remain to the casual observer had there actually been one.

Did this lifetime of pilfering money from good-faith employers ever bother Sydney Bridgewater's conscience?

Did she ever feel guilty of wrong-doing on some level?

Answer: No, she did not. It was a contest of wits to her; she'd been smarter and had come out ahead.

But how had she managed to steal so many millions over so many years and never get caught?

How had she gone blissfully month to month as cash accumulated into now a huge heap without anyone finding out? Every wrong-doer is eventually apprehended, right?

Answer: she avoided notice through simple common sense.

She planned each incident expertly, methodically, and carefully.

Her code operated invisibly, cleaned up after itself, and left no crumbs behind to follow.

She was patient, content with taking small amounts steadily rather than risking everything for a big score.

She lived simply, calling no attention to herself with outrageous, overly visible purchases.

And most important, she kept her mouth shut, never bragging about how smart she was to fool everyone.

She was an intelligent, creative, devious, lovable, and unlikely thief.

But always a thief.

It was how she liked it.

Juliana called Austin several weeks after his bonus letter arrived. He was out delivering packages but answered right away.

"We're inviting you to play Monopoly with us at The Board Room tomorrow night," she said. "Interested?"

"Definitely. I haven't had a good hot dog since the last time I was there, which was, I believe, yesterday."

"Perfect. See you around six, okay?" He agreed.

So, he sat down the following evening, ordered a heaping bowl of potato chips and a hot dog with spicy mustard and onions, and began a real estate battle with Caroline, David, and Juliana. The play was spirited and most enjoyable. Sandra and Rory kept everyone supplied with food and frequently commented on the game's progress. Becky motored by often with more chips, and she and Sandra and Rory substituted now and then when a player wanted a break.

At some point, Austin asked a question that had been on his mind.

"Whatever became of the big lawsuit those property buyers filed? I haven't seen news of it anywhere."

"C. Monica filled us in," Caroline said. "They're still going back and forth and would do so forever except for one thing: the individuals who originally filed the suit can't pay their attorneys. It's the kiss of death, of course, so the whole case will likely fall flat fairly soon. The follow-on suit she mentioned never happened and likely won't."

"That sounds good. I'm sure it's a relief for you," Austin said. "Um, I have another question. You don't have to answer if you'd rather not."

"Just ask," said Juliana.

"After dealing with those parcels – hiding them originally, helping you find them 11 years later – I've always been curious about what was actually in them."

"Did you come up with any good guesses?"

"Nothing specific, but I figured since your dad wanted them opened in sequence. Together they must tell some sort of story. Did they tell a story?"

"They did," Caroline said. "There was cash, jewelry, a couple of books, safe deposit box keys, a ton of documents, and finally dad's actual will. Though it took a while for all the parts to come together, it finally did tell a story."

"It was a story we didn't know we needed to hear, but now we're glad we did," Juliana added. "Thanks for your part in making it happen."

"You're welcome. It was an excellent adventure."

The Monopoly battle raged on but no one matched David, a man with strategy.

He had years of experience playing 37 different game versions with Becky.

He was the down-the-field, nobody-near-him winner.

"I understand you still live in the same apartment as when you started burying those parcels long ago," he said.

"I do," Austin replied. "It's comfortable and I don't accumulate stuff, or maybe I get rid of stuff at about the same rate as I bring new stuff in."

"We have a proposition for you," said Caroline, "and we're hoping you'll be interested."

"Sure, tell me about it."

"Dad left his house, the one we all grew up in, to the three of us," Caroline continued. "We can live in it, sell it, tear it down, whatever the three of us agree to.

"None of us wants to move there. We have homes wholly paid for, we're happy in them, and relocating only to be somewhere else is too much bother.

"We don't want to get rid of it in any way because it's part of our history. But it does require maintenance. Service companies regularly come to clean and tend the yard and check the mechanics, of course, but we'd like someone to be there.

"So, we've agreed to this proposal: how would you like to live there?"

"Whoa," Austin said, "it's a big place for one person."

"It is," Juliana said, "but it's completely furnished, and our Estate pays expenses every month as long as we still own it. You'd be like a permanent caretaker with a no-expense home."

"It would be a major upgrade of neighborhood for me, for sure," Austin replied. "I'm going to say yes, I'm interested."

"Great," David said. "We've set aside a couple of rooms and stored mom's and dad's and our things there, so the house is ready to go. Oh, and it comes with some clunky vintage thing that hasn't been out of the garage in years. We'll give it to you to drive or sell or junk, whatever you wish."

"Now for sure, I'm interested."

"Then it's a deal," Caroline said. "I'll have C. Monica draw up any paperwork needed and you can move in when you like."

"Thank you all very much," Austin said.

He moved to his new neighborhood three weeks later. He packed personal belongings he wanted to keep, left furniture behind and a few boxes of junk on the curb, then headed to what was undoubtedly "uptown."

When fully settled in a month later and enjoying his new surroundings, he finally opened the garage. The "clunky vintage thing" David mentioned turned out to be a 1986 Lincoln Town Car Cartier, worth anywhere from $10,000 to $25,000 depending on its condition and who was selling it. Austin checked it out thoroughly.

Oh, no, he definitely wouldn't sell it.

Junk it? Terrible idea.

Instead, after complete restoration it would become a classy, brand-new, for-hire limousine.

A new business opportunity had suddenly appeared fully formed in his mind. It had probably been waiting there for months and only needed sufficient time on The Road to give it final form.

Oklahoma City was full of companies and hundreds of executives. With a stylish chauffeur's outfit, he'd soon become the limousine driver most often requested taking clients wherever they chose. The tagline lettered on his beautifully restored Lincoln would tell his story:

Austin Somerfeld Limo

Nowhere to go but everywhere

After all, he was famous.

He delivered.

– The End –